"CAN YOU READ MY MIND RIGHT NOW?" NATE ASKED.

"Not unless we're touching, and even then, not a hundred percent. If it makes you feel any better, I've read your mind quite a bit over the last few days—"

"Oh, yeah, feeling better already." What had he thought? What did Tess know about him?

"And," she continued doggedly, "I haven't picked up one single thing that made me uncomfortable. That's a first. In fact, I'd even started to think . . ." She stopped, unable to continue, as her face turned a becoming shade of pink.

He couldn't stand it. He had to touch her. She knew what he was thinking anyhow, right? And all he wanted was to be closer. . . .

She didn't flinch or pull away, but leaned closer when he pulled her gently into his lap. He brought her lips to his. His mind filled with all sorts of sensual images he was helpless to stop, so he didn't even try..

"Mm-hmm," she murmured as her arms stole around his neck. "Oh, yes."

Was she sharing his thoughts, or just approving of the way he rubbed her back?

"Both," she whispered.

WHAT ARE *LOVESWEPT* ROMANCES?

They are stories of true romance and touching emotion. We believe those two very important ingredients are constants in our highly sensual and very believable stories in the LOVE-SWEPT line. Our goal is to give you, the reader, stories of consistently high quality that may sometimes make you laugh, sometimes make you cry, but are always fresh and creative and contain many delightful surprises within their pages.

Most romance fans read an enormous number of books. Those they truly love, they keep. Others may be traded with friends and soon forgotten. We hope that each LOVESWEPT romance will be a treasure—a "keeper." We will always try to publish

LOVE STORIES YOU'LL NEVER FORGET
BY AUTHORS YOU'LL ALWAYS REMEMBER

The Editors

WITCHY WOMAN

KAREN LEABO

BANTAM BOOKS

NEW YORK · TORONTO · LONDON · SYDNEY · AUCKLAND

WITCHY WOMAN

A Bantam Book / June 1998

ISBN 0-553-44652-5

Published simultaneously in the United States and Canada

Bantam Books are published by Bantam Books, a division of Bantam Dou-
bleday Dell Publishing Group, Inc. Its trademark, consisting of the words
"Bantam Books" and the portrayal of a rooster, is Registered in U.S.
Patent and Trademark Office and in other countries. Marca Registrada.
Bantam Books, 1540 Broadway, New York, New York 10036.

PRINTED IN THE UNITED STATES OF AMERICA

OPM   10 9 8 7 6 5 4 3 2 1

Dear Reader:

Another year has gone by—I can't believe it! I was tickled pink to find out that WITCHY WOMAN would be a part of Loveswept's Extraordinary Lovers theme month. I was doubly tickled when I found out that Extraordinary Lovers coincided with Loveswept's 15th Anniversary. That's two good reasons to celebrate.

WITCHY WOMAN is a special book for me. It's a challenge to take a fantastic subject, in this case a statue with an evil gypsy curse, and make it sound believable. I think it helps me, though, that I believe in magic.

I've always been drawn to other-worldly things. Alas, I'm nowhere near as sensitive as my heroine, Tess. But I'm still fascinated by the possibilities. You can bet the other three June Loveswepts will find themselves instantly at the top of my huge to-be-read pile.

The second kind of magic I believe in is love, which is why I found it so much fun to weave witch's spells and love together.

Speaking of love, I found it in real life. I got married last Christmas Eve to a great guy, which just goes to show, you never know where or when love will turn up. I found Rob at a romance writers' meeting, and though I don't often dedicate my books, this one's for him.

I sincerely hope you enjoy WITCHY WOMAN. And here's to 15 more years of Loveswept!

All my best,

Karen Leabo

ONE

She didn't look anything like a witch.

That was the first thing that struck Nate Wagner when he finally got a good look at the woman he was following. In fact, with her short, wispy blond hair and sea-blue eyes big enough to swim in, Tess DeWitt reminded him more of a siren than a sorceress.

His reporter's brain made quick, mental notes on her appearance: medium height, slim build, great legs. Kissable mouth.

He quickly deleted that last attribute from his list. He wasn't interested in sex; he was interested in a great story.

Or maybe not. His informant had to be wrong, Nate decided as he trailed a discreet distance behind the woman, who casually licked an ice-cream cone while she ambled along the sidewalk of a fashionable Back Bay street with a friend. This lovely woman with the come-hither eyes could not be the notorious

Moonbeam Majick, the child witch who fifteen years earlier had captured the attention of Boston and then scared the whole town silly.

Nate remembered the incident clearly, although at eighteen he'd been scarcely more than a child himself. "Moonbeam," a skinny, prepubescent girl with wary, suspicious eyes and long black hair, had been a popular guest on a local talk show. Appearing with her mother, Morganna Majick, Moonbeam had been billed as the most gifted young psychic in the country. And indeed, her on-air mind-reading performances had been impressive, although most people, including Nate, dismissed them as parlor tricks.

Then one day during her routine she had stopped mid-sentence and treated the show's host, one Don Woodland, to a piercing stare that gave him and everyone who had been watching a case of the willies. "Be careful going home today," she'd intoned mournfully before continuing with her routine.

That evening, as he'd crossed the street on his way to the subway station, Don Woodland had been killed by a hit-and-run driver.

Moonbeam's "amazing prediction" was in the headlines for several days as she and her mother were swamped with demands for psychic readings. Not everyone was so favorably impressed, however. Some angry citizens, most notably the family of Don Woodland, had demanded an investigation, hinting that perhaps Don's tragic end was no accident. Others, even more hysterical, accused Moonbeam of putting a witch's curse on Woodland. They called her a devil worshiper and suggested she should be put away.

Subsequently there had been an investigation—not by the police, but by the Department of Family Services. Someone had complained that Morganna was no fit mother. At the very least, Morganna had been practicing devilish magic of some sort, as indicated by the pentagrams, black candles, and other more sordid evidence uncovered in her house, and she'd been indoctrinating her daughter into the practice as well. Moonbeam had been removed from her mother's custody, and no one had heard a word about her ever again.

Until now.

A friend of Nate's, Barbara Kirkland, had tipped him off. The notorious Moonbeam was actually Tess DeWitt, a seemingly innocuous product manager who worked for the software company where Barbara was a secretary. Nate figured it would make a good story— "Whatever Happened to Moonbeam Majick?" The editor of *Boston Life* magazine had told him to go for it. If it turned out to be interesting and sensational enough, Nate might even be able to sell it to a national publication.

But first he had to gain the cooperation of Tess DeWitt—if she was indeed Moonbeam, which he really doubted now that he'd seen her.

The two women paused to look in the window of an antique shop. Nate strolled by them, listening to their conversation. As he passed Tess he got a whiff of the most delicate, indescribable scent. He inhaled deeply, wanting a second helping, but all he got was a noseful of exhaust from a passing car.

"I can't go inside holding an ice-cream cone," Tess said to her friend, a tall woman with an outlandish hat perched atop her short red hair.

"Well, come inside when you finish," the friend said. "I need you to help me pick out a birthday gift for my aunt Dora. You're always so good at knowing what people like."

"You know, Judy, this shop has the highest prices in town," Tess admonished with a shake of her head. Her hair, which caught the brisk autumn breeze and fluffed up around her face, fell back into place in an artfully windswept order that Nate had seldom seen in real life—only in the pages of magazines.

"Price isn't everything," the woman named Judy replied.

Nate paused near the two women, pretending interest in a collection of old dolls that sat in the antique shop's front window. From the corner of his eye he watched as the redhead went inside, leaving Tess alone. Tess didn't seem to mind. She finished her strawberry ice cream with sensual abandon, biting off the end of the cone and tipping back her head to catch the last few pink drips. Then she threw the rest away and delicately wiped her mouth and fingertips with a paper napkin.

"Are you interested in dolls?" she asked.

Nate's head jerked around. "Uh, yeah. Well, no, not for me." Way to go, Wagner. She'd caught him loitering. Quickly he improvised some cover. "I was thinking about my older sister, though. She had a baby a few weeks ago, and now she's feeling kind of down. I thought a present might perk her up." The story was true, for the most part. "She likes dolls." Or she had when she'd been six years old.

Tess walked over and stood beside him so that she could study the collection of dolls herself. This close to her, Nate could catalog additional traits: skin like fine china, a neck impossibly slim and graceful, breasts that were neither large nor small, but softly rounded and natural looking beneath her cream silk blouse.

"Hmm, I'm afraid I don't know anything about antique dolls," Tess said, "but the one on the far left is pretty."

"Yeah, I guess. Maybe I'll go in to have a look at her." He moved toward the door, but Tess didn't follow his lead. "Are you coming inside?"

She made an obvious grimace. "Might as well." He opened the door, which announced their entrance with a cheerful jingle of bells, and she stepped in ahead of him.

The store, which was crowded with furniture, glassware, and knickknacks of every description, smelled strongly of lemon oil and lavender, not an unpleasant combination. Nate watched with interest as Tess closed her eyes and took a deep breath, as if acclimating herself to some rarefied foreign environment. She didn't appear comfortable.

"Tess, I'm over here," the redhead called, waving from across the store. "Look at this wonderful Chinese vase I found."

Tess went to join her friend, leaving Nate to figure

out how he was going to pursue his acquaintance with her. He had already decided on the best approach for his story: He would get to know her first, then ease into the subject of the occult and see if she nibbled. Then he would act as if he'd only just that moment thought of writing a story about her. Not entirely aboveboard, perhaps, but he had scared away more than one sensitive source by being too up-front.

Noticing another group of dolls closer to where the two women were chatting about a rather ordinary-looking blue-glazed vase, he ambled over.

"Three hundred dollars seems a lot to pay for a cracked vase, Ming dynasty or not," Tess was saying.

"But it's so old—almost four hundred years!"

"Hmm. I don't know. . . ." Tentatively she touched the vase, again closing her eyes and taking a deep breath. "No," she said decisively. "I'm sure your aunt Dora wouldn't like this piece. How about . . ."

She quickly scanned the shop's contents until her gaze caught abruptly on something very near Nate. He thought she was staring at him, until he realized the focus of her attention was something above and behind him.

He turned to see what it was. There, sitting in a place of honor on the top shelf of a massive bookcase, was a stone figurine of a jungle cat of some sort, a panther, maybe, crouched as if ready to pounce. The stone was red—deep, dark, bloodred—and the cat had iridescent yellow stones for eyes. It was quite a striking piece.

"I don't believe it," she murmured as she came closer.

Nate stepped aside to give her access. Then, realizing the statue was up too high for her, he reached toward it himself, intending to bring it down for her closer inspection.

"Don't touch it!" she cautioned, but it was too late. The figurine was already in his hands.

It was heavy, and warmer than cold stone should have felt. "What's wrong?" he asked as she backed away from it. "I thought you wanted to see it."

"P-put it back," she said. Her huge blue eyes clearly revealed her dread.

Judy, who had come up behind Tess, was apparently as confused as Nate. "Why?" she asked. "That's a beautiful statue. How much is it? I think my aunt Dora would love it. It's Chinese, isn't it?"

Nate looked on the bottom. The price seemed very reasonable, considering the tags he'd noticed on some of the other items. "It's fifty dollars," he told Judy.

"Perfect," Judy exclaimed, reaching for the statue.

"No!" Tess barked. "Judy, listen to me. Your aunt Dora would hate that statue. Trust me on this one."

"But you don't even know my aunt Dora."

"I know what old ladies like, and that statue is all wrong for an old lady."

By now their heated words had drawn the attention of the store's proprietor, who had been seated behind a rolltop desk attending to some kind of busywork. She hobbled over, using a cane because her entire left leg was encased in a cast, a pinched expression on her thin, aristocratic face.

"May I be of some assistance?" she asked, peeking over the top of her reading glasses. Then her gaze fell on the statue in Nate's hands. "Oh, I see you've found one of my favorite pieces."

"Where did you get it?" Tess demanded without even a semblance of polite curiosity.

The proprietor, whose name tag identified her as Anne-Louise Morrell, didn't seem to notice. "A young gentleman brought it into the store one day. He seemed quite anxious to part with it, though I'm not sure why, and he wasn't particular about compensation. I paid him a pittance for it—that's why I was able to price it so low." She paused, looking expectantly from face to face.

"How old is it?" Judy asked.

Anne-Louise was only too happy to wax enthusiastic. "Oh, it's very old. I can't say for sure when or where it originated, but have you ever seen the carved figures displayed at the palace of Versailles? This one is very similar."

I'll just bet, Nate thought. And if the expression on Tess's face was any indication, her thoughts were running along the same skeptical track. Still, the statue was worth fifty bucks for aesthetic value alone, never mind its value as an antique. If this Judy didn't buy it, he just might.

He set the statue on a tabletop, intending to let Judy have a better look at it. As he pulled his hand away he scratched his finger on a sharp edge—the panther's back claws. A drop of blood welled up on his fingertip.

Tess, her attention glued to his every move, grew pale at the sight. "Oh, my God . . ."

"It's nothing," he said in an effort to alleviate her unwarranted distress. "Just a nick." He shoved his sore finger into his mouth.

Without further ado she grabbed her friend's arm in a death grip. "I saw a beautiful lamp at Filene's that your aunt would love," she said in an insistent voice. "We can go tomorrow and look at it. But now we'd better leave, or we'll be late getting back to work. Good-bye, and thank you." Her nod included both Nate and Anne-Louise as she dragged a befuddled Judy out the door.

"Well, how odd," the shopkeeper said. "I can't tell you how many people have expressed an interest in that piece and then changed their minds. I've dropped the price on it twice. If I go any lower, I won't make a profit at all."

"Anxious to get rid of it, are you?"

She shrugged noncommittally. "I'm actually rather fond of it," she admitted, "but I'd never make a living in this business if I kept every piece I took a fancy to."

Nate, still inclined to purchase the panther even after it had scratched him, picked it up gingerly and replaced it on the high shelf. Maybe after he got paid for the Moonbeam Majick story, he'd come back and buy the piece as a reward.

"I noticed you were interested in the dolls," Anne-

Louise said. "Could I show you any from the window?"

"Ah, no, not today." He was wondering whether he should try to catch up to Tess and talk to her. But what would he say? Rather than risk irritating her, he decided to wait for another day. He could easily stage a coincidental meeting of some sort. "How did you break your leg?" he impulsively asked the shopkeeper. He'd never been shy about expressing his curiosity.

"Oh, it was the silliest thing," she said. "It was the same day I bought the statue, as a matter of fact. I remember because I decided to run upstairs to my storage room for some reference books, to see if I could figure out what on earth I'd bought. And on the way down, I just tripped over my own two clumsy feet. I'll bet you I've been up and down those stairs a million times over the nine years I've owned this shop, and I've never tripped before. Silliest thing."

Nate wasn't sure why, but Anne-Louise's explanation gave him an odd, unsettled feeling in his gut. "I'd better be going too," he said to the woman, although he wondered if he might not buy a doll for his sister after all.

When he exited the store he was surprised to find Tess and her friend still in sight. They stood in the middle of the sidewalk half a block up, apparently arguing.

". . . because that vase was no more antique than the ones you can buy at Wal-Mart, that's why," Tess was saying.

Nate stood transfixed, marveling at the sight of Tess

in the throes of a passionate opinion. She was a fiercely magnificent creature.

"How do you know?" Judy retorted. "You don't even like antiques. And the stone cat? What was wrong with it?"

"You don't want that thing in your possession, not even for a minute," Tess insisted. "It's . . ." She lowered her voice. "It looks evil."

Judy stared as her face reflected disbelief, then acceptance. "All right," she said, suddenly subdued.

Nate saw his chance and made his move. "Excuse me, ladies, but I couldn't help overhearing."

"It's hard not to overhear when you're eavesdropping," Tess said, although she softened the comment with a crooked smile.

Nate spread his hands in a gesture of surrender, trying his best to be disarming. "Guilty as charged. But it's an occupational hazard. I'm a freelance writer, working at the moment for *Boston Life*. Nate Wagner." He held out his hand to Judy, who seemed the more receptive of the two.

Judy shook his hand warmly. "I'm Judy Cosgrove, and my suspicious friend here is Tess DeWitt. What are you working on, a story about how corporate women spend their lunch hours?"

Not a bad idea, he thought, filing it away for later. "Actually, I'm doing an investigative piece on antique shops," he improvised. "I understand there's quite a lot of deception that goes on—faked authenticity certificates, price gouging, bilking the unwary customer, that sort of thing." Another not-so-bad idea. If nothing else, he'd come away from today's adventure with some story ideas to pitch to various editors. "And I just wanted to ask . . ."—he turned to Tess—"you, the suspicious one—Tess, did you say?"

She nodded, arms crossed under those perfectly medium-sized breasts, as if she wasn't buying a word of it.

"How do you know the vase isn't a real antique?"

She shrugged. "I saw one just like it in another shop, same crack and everything."

"Really? Which shop?" He was liking this crooked-antique-dealer story more and more.

"I don't remember," she replied with a toss of her head, making her hair dance again. He liked her hair. It was a natural honey-and-sunshine color that couldn't have come out of a bottle. That weird, black-haired kid he'd seen on TV all those years ago could never have grown up into this fair, delicate creature.

"Well, if you do remember, or if you hear of any horror stories concerning antique dealers, I wish you'd give me a call." He handed both women his card. Tess handled hers gingerly by the edges, dropping it into an outer pocket of her vinyl purse. He was hoping she might reciprocate with a card of her own, giving him legitimate means to call her, but she didn't.

Judy, however, did. "I love antiques, but I'm always paying too much for things," she said. "I can't tell you how many times Tess has saved me from a tragically ignorant impulse buy. I know all the shops—which ones overcharge the most, which ones offer bargains. If you'll call me later, I'll tell you what I know."

"Thanks. I'll do that."

"Oh, Mr. Wagner?" It was Tess who spoke up, surprising him.

"Please, call me Nate."

She fixed him with a stare, her eyes holding an otherworldly intensity. "Do be careful."

A chill snaked its way up his spine. "Excuse me?"

And then she seemed perfectly normal again. "You should be more careful when you handle old things in antique shops. That cut on your finger—no telling what kind of germs you picked up. You should wash it out with alcohol as soon as possible."

"Yes, yes, I'll do that." Had he only imagined that fleeting strangeness about her? As he watched the two women walk away from him, he suddenly knew, beyond a doubt, that Tess DeWitt was in fact Moonbeam Majick.

At five minutes until five, Tess sat at her desk with her head in her hands, utterly drained. If she had to take one more phone call or track down one more glitch in one more program, she would go mad. What she needed was a bath—a long, hot, blessedly isolating bath. The tub seemed to be the only place she could empty her mind and achieve total relaxation.

The tension was worse than usual after her unnerving lunch hour.

Despite the constant battle of dealing with her "gift," she didn't think much about the old days anymore. Fifteen years was a long time, and she'd forgotten most of the events prior to her thirteenth birthday. The nightmares had stopped years before, and the image of her mother's face was only a blur in her mind, so infrequently had they seen each other in recent years. But seeing that blasted red panther had brought it all crashing back.

She'd only been a child when she'd last seen the statue. But there couldn't be two pieces so alike. Besides, she had felt the evil emanating from that unholy cat. Without her even touching it, the vibrations had reached toward her like a blackened, skeletal hand reaching from the grave.

She had no doubt in her mind that the Crimson Cat could kill. As a child, she had watched her uncle sicken and die less than a month after finding the statue in his attic among her grandmother's effects. She remembered overhearing whispers about a curse and, little by little, piecing together the story.

Apparently a Gypsy woman who practiced dark magic had placed the curse on the cat statue a couple of hundred years ago, then had vindictively given the cat to Tess's great-great-grandmother, a white witch. The curse had proved so powerful that it had been passed from generation to generation, ending with Tess's mother.

Tess shivered as she recalled the transformation that had taken place, the stranger her mother had become after she had inherited the statue. In Morganna Majick's case, death would have been a kinder fate.

It was rumored that even casual possession of the statue—holding it, or touching it—could cause bad luck. To actually own it invited disaster. And the more one valued the cat, the worse that luck became.

Tess thought back to the shopkeeper and her broken leg. She would bet her last dollar the accident had occurred after Anne-Louise had acquired the statue. And the cut on Nate Wagner's finger. No coincidence, that.

Nate Wagner. A strange warmth flooded her as she rolled his name around in her mind.

She'd noticed him right away, standing by that window and pretending to look at the dolls when all the while he was eyeing her, and his covert attention had given her a small thrill of feminine delight. After all, how often was it that a tall, dark, and rakishly handsome man looked at her twice? Or rather, how often had she allowed it?

She had recognized his story about his sister for the subterfuge it was, and had forgiven him for it. Her ego, she supposed, had wanted to paint him as a good guy. It wasn't any fun to flirt with a slimeball.

But then there had been that business with the Crimson Cat, and all she'd wanted was to get out of that shop. A part of her—an unfamiliar part—had wanted to linger with the appealing stranger, but raw fear had won out and she'd fled. Only when she'd seen him again outside, in the sunlight, had she admitted that she might have overreacted a bit.

He was undeniably sexy, even in worn corduroys and an old windbreaker that should have seen the inside of a garbage can years before. He had a lean face with a prominent, almost hawkish nose and warm brown eyes. His hair, wild and curly and brown like his eyes, blatantly defied conventional styling.

Of course, when he'd told her and Judy what he was up to, she had realized that his interest in her hadn't been personal. That hadn't stopped her from feeling a strange, sensual pull toward him. She shivered with delight at the memory.

She hoped a cut finger was the worst that would come of his brush with the curse. But as she'd held his business card ever so gingerly, she had felt the aura of danger that surrounded him. She'd given him the best warning she could under the circumstances. Anything stronger, and he would have dismissed her as a nut.

She wondered if there was any other precaution she could take for his benefit.

His card was in her purse. Though she seldom deliberately called on her extrasensory abilities, this time she really had no choice. It was her fault that Nate Wagner had touched the cat in the first place. If she hadn't seen it and stared at it with her mouth gaping open, he wouldn't even have noticed the statue. She owed him this small bit of effort.

She plucked the card from her purse and studied it: NATHANIEL WAGNER, FREELANCE WRITER. An address in Cambridge. Next she held the card between her clasped hands, closed her eyes, and took a deep breath.

The first sensations to hit her mind were comfortable ones, like a warm breeze on a languorous summer day, adding to her favorable impression of the man. But, gradually, the comfortable feeling became less so. Warmth turned to heat, languor to need, and the breeze became a caress, a human caress. She felt his touch against her face, on her neck, her breasts. . . .

She wrenched her eyes open and the vision disintegrated. "Good gravy," she muttered. That sort of information was hardly pertinent. Unfortunately her powers were unpredictable at best. The sensitivity was almost always there, whenever she came into physical contact with a person or thing, but Tess had no control over which vibrations she received when.

She cleared her mind, took a deep breath, closed her eyes, and tried again.

There was a crowd pressing against her from all sides, and a roar reverberating in her ears. A sudden shove, the sensation of falling . . . panic, a mad scramble for safety, a hot wind that brought near death and—

A sharp tap on her door and *pop!* The vision was gone.

The door opened and Judy stuck her head inside the office. "Aren't you ready to go home yet?"

Tess glanced at her watch. It was already five-twenty. Quickly she thrust Nate's business card back into her purse. "Come on in. I was just finishing up." She began stuffing papers into her briefcase, papers she probably wouldn't even look at once she got home. But executives at her place of employment always carried briefcases. It was part of the uniform, as were the conservative suit and low-key jewelry.

"Hey, Tess," Judy began in a low voice, "I'm sorry about hassling you today."

"Hassling me?"

"Outside the antique store. I realized, too late, why you were upset."

If Judy knew why she was upset, Tess would have to give her friend credit for a few psychic abilities of her own.

"That panther statue," Judy continued. "Did it remind you of something from your past?"

Hmm, not a bad guess. Judy was Tess's closest friend, and thus one of a select handful who knew about her past as Moonbeam. But even Judy knew only the barest facts about Tess's nightmarish childhood. The only people who had known the whole truth were a social worker, since transferred to another city, a kindly judge, who had died years earlier, and the psychiatrist she had seen during her teenage years.

And her mother, of course.

Even her aunt, who'd ended up as Tess's dutiful but distant guardian, didn't know how bizarre life with Morganna had become toward the end.

"Yes, it did bring back the past," Tess answered. "I know my behavior must seem irrational to you." Judy, while entirely sympathetic to the hardships Tess had endured, didn't believe in anything remotely supernatural. That was one of the reasons Tess liked her so much. She didn't have to hide her abilities around Judy, because Judy would never believe in them anyway.

"It's okay," Judy said, dismissing the apology with a wave of her hand. "Anyway, you were right. Aunt Dora doesn't even like cats. Come on, let's get going. I have an aerobics class to get to."

Per long-standing arrangement, Tess walked Judy to her car, then Judy dropped Tess off at the Copley Square T station.

As soon as Tess pushed her way through the turnstile, it hit her. The subway! That was the atmosphere she'd sensed in her vision. Now she wished she had taken the time earlier to relax with Nate's business card. Maybe she could have encouraged him to take a cab or something. Because what she'd seen in her mind's eye had already taken place. She knew it.

TWO

Tess breathed a sigh of relief after she closed and bolted the front door of her condo in South Boston, her personal refuge. The vibrations she'd dealt with during the day had been particularly taxing.

Most unsettling had been her run-in with Nate Wagner—both physically and mentally. His bodily presence had done wild things to her restless hormones. But the vision she'd experienced when holding his business card . . . Just by closing her eyes, she could vividly relive those fleeting, exquisite images that suggested a future sexual encounter.

She kept her eyes resolutely open as she hung her purse on a hook by the door and kicked off her shoes. She ordered herself to focus instead on the pleasure of being home.

She had scrimped and saved for years to buy this two-bedroom, split-level town house. The building was brand-new, made of clean stucco with a Spanish-tiled roof, oddly out of place in Boston, but she liked it anyway—especially the commanding view of the ocean.

She wiggled her stockinged toes against the plush white carpet. Most everything she owned had been purchased new when she'd moved in, from the white furniture, to the pictures on the white walls, to the snowy sheets and towels that touched her body so intimately. She hadn't yet found a place completely free of the psychic vibrations that plagued her, but this was as close as she'd ever come. This was her haven.

Tess still intended to have that hot soak in the tub. But first there was the matter of Nate Wagner. She would have to call him, or she would drive herself crazy wondering what had happened to him on the subway.

She took the card out of her purse again and sat on her sofa, leaning back against the pastel silk pillows. She didn't consciously seek vibrations from the card, but a few reached her nonetheless. This time she got a distinct impression of deception—not an evil or malicious sort of lie, but a mild omission of the whole truth. Nate Wagner, apparently, hadn't represented himself with a hundred-percent honesty. Interesting.

She dialed his number, her heart thumping wildly. The phone rang once, twice. Come on, she thought. Please, be okay. Despite her apprehension, she was actually breathless at the idea of talking to him again.

He answered the phone on the fourth ring.

She was unbearably relieved to hear his voice. Whatever bad luck had transpired, he was still alive. "Hi, this is Tess DeWitt. From the antique store?"

"Yes. Hello, Tess." He sounded both surprised and

pleased to hear from her. "Did you remember where you saw that other vase?"

Oh, yeah, the vase. She had lied to him too. She didn't like lying, but sometimes it was a necessity. He wouldn't have understood if she'd told him the truth—that the instant she'd touched the cool, artificially aged porcelain of the "Ming" vase, she had seen a sweatshop in the Philippines where those vases had been manufactured en masse no more than two years before.

"No, I really don't remember," she said.

"Oh." She could almost hear what he didn't say: Then why are you calling?

"Actually, the reason I called is . . ." She thought about telling him of her premonition that the two of them would become lovers. Depending on how much the idea appealed to him, he might or might not accept her ridiculous explanation. ". . . because I was wondering," she said instead, her words coming totally from impulse. "Do you want any help with your antiques story?"

"What kind of help?"

"Well, I'm no expert or anything, but I do know most of the shops, and sometimes I can distinguish a reproduction from the real thing. I might also be able to point out some of the more ridiculously overpriced items. Would that be helpful?" What was she doing? she thought in a mild panic. Making a date? Was that smart? Was that sane? Was she trying to bring on a self-fulfilling prophecy?

"As a matter of fact, it would. But your friend said you didn't like antiques."

"I don't happen to have any in my own home, but I still appreciate their quality and beauty." As long as she didn't have to touch them a great deal. "Are you interested?" Why was she doing this to herself? She was uncomfortable around old things; the older the object, the more vibrations it stored.

"Sure. How soon can we get together? You could bring Judy too. Sounds like she might have some interesting anecdotes to get me started."

Tess was a bit disappointed that he'd requested extra company. But he probably wasn't interested in her as a woman, she reminded herself. Maybe the "vision" she'd had was nothing more than the fantasies of a frustrated, twenty-eight-year-old virgin who in all likelihood would remain a virgin, until someone invented a way to make love without prolonged touching.

"I've committed myself to help Judy pick out a gift for her aunt Dora on Saturday," Tess said brightly, "but maybe we could meet you afterward—say around one o'clock?"

"Great. How about in front of that same store?"

"No," she said quickly. She didn't want to go anywhere near that shop. "There's a store on Newbury Street called the Picket Fence, at the corner of Gloucester. Horrendous prices. Let's start there."

"Sounds good."

Tess realized the conversation was quickly winding down, and she still hadn't achieved her true purpose. "How's your finger? Did you wash out the cut?"

"The cut was so tiny, I couldn't even find it when I

got home. I appreciate the concern, but I don't think you need to worry about gangrene."

He was teasing her, but in such a good-natured way that she actually enjoyed it. "You can never be too careful," she said. "I had an uncle who once got a splinter in his toe. He ignored it, and they ended up amputating his foot. Danger can lurk in the most unlikely places."

"Hey, no kidding. I almost got killed in a T station today."

"Really?" She was relieved at how easy it had been to manipulate the conversation. "What happened?"

"There were a bunch of people waiting for the next train. When it came into view, this nutcase bulldozed his way through the crowd, knocking people over right and left, screaming something about being first to board. I got pushed onto the track right in front of the train. If I hadn't scrambled back out of that pit in a hurry, I would've been dog food."

Tess shivered as the scraps of her vision took on a new meaning. "Thank goodness you have quick reflexes," she said. The memory of Mr. Woodland, the talk-show host, and his tragic end came suddenly, uncomfortably to mind. He had touched her shoulder, and she had immediately envisioned the accident. She'd always regretted that she hadn't given him a better, more specific warning.

Not that he would have believed her. He had enjoyed having her as a guest on his show, but he'd been a total skeptic.

Tess quickly concluded her conversation with Nate,

worried that in her present state of mind she might slip and reveal something she would rather keep to herself.

When she was alone with just the silence around her, she once again held Nate's card between her hands. She was suddenly voraciously curious about him. This time, however, she felt absolutely nothing, indicating she had already sensed all the stored information that was hers to receive from this particular object.

It was probably just as well. It wasn't fair for her to learn things about Nate with extrasensory methods when he couldn't do the same with her. She resolved that she'd have to glean any other information she wanted about him in the ordinary way.

Nate couldn't believe his good luck. He had asked Tess to bring Judy along on their antiquing jaunt because he hadn't wanted Tess to feel pressured or uneasy. He was going to play this little fish very carefully. But as it turned out, Judy was busy with something else. Nate had Tess to himself for the entire afternoon.

He couldn't even hint, of course, that he harbored anything but a professional interest in her knowledge of antiques—although he did. The more he talked to her, the more he saw of her, the more he was drawn to her.

Maybe it was a good thing he couldn't act on his attraction. How wise was it, after all, to become involved with a witch?

She looked even less witchlike than she had at their

first meeting. Wearing a fuzzy, oversized lavender sweater that skimmed her thighs, white corduroy jeans, and lavender canvas sneakers, she presented a whole-some-but-sexy image that made him want to protect her and seduce her all at the same time.

But she was Moonbeam, of that he was sure. The warning she'd given him as they'd stood on the side-walk had been enough to send a shiver down his spine; almost getting squashed by a subway train not twenty minutes later had been downright spooky.

Not that he believed in psychic stuff. But he did believe in subconscious suggestion. His own careless-ness no doubt had caused the near accident, careless-ness brought on by his preoccupation with the warning.

He wondered if Don Woodland, too, had been rat-tled by Moonbeam's stark admonition, so rattled that he'd walked out in front of a car. That might be an interesting angle to explore.

"Have you eaten?" he asked Tess as they browsed among the fussy-looking displays at the Picket Fence. He noticed that although she looked at things with lively attention, she held her slender hands behind her back, rarely touching anything.

"Now that you mention it, Judy and I got so in-volved with the shopping that we forgot to eat. I'm famished."

"There's a great sandwich shop across the street. Let me buy you lunch. I'll charge it off to the maga-zine—professional consulting fee."

She laughed at that. "Some consultant. I haven't

found anything interesting for your story except some slightly overpriced furniture."

"Hey, we've only just started. Who knows, in the next store we might find a fake Chippendale or a forged Picasso lithograph."

"Uh-huh." She looked skeptically down her aristocratic little nose at him—as best she could, since he was almost a head taller than she was. Then she laughed again.

Her laughter caused a pleasurable sensation to ripple down his spine and settle in a more provocative area. How could mere laughter have that much kick? he wondered as they headed out into the bright October sunshine and crossed Newbury.

The street was crowded with shoppers eager to sample the finery inside the many pricey boutiques. The sandwich shop was crowded, too, and Nate and Tess waited in line at the counter for several minutes. He stood close enough behind her that he could smell her hair. Fascinated by the light, herbal fragrance, he was on the verge of asking her what shampoo she used.

His decision not to act on his attraction was rapidly crumbling.

Finally the woman behind the counter was ready to take their order. Despite Nate's insistence that Tess splurge on whatever she wanted, she limited herself to a grilled-cheese sandwich, a cup of tomato soup, and mineral water. Surely she wasn't dieting, he thought. She was already so slender, he could easily span her waist with his hands. That little bit of imagery did nothing to bolster his resolve.

"So," she said when they finally were seated at a table by the window, "what else do you know about phony antiques?"

Nate was ready for this one. He had actually done some reading on the subject, and he was half-serious about writing the story. "It's a big racket right now, and often as not, the shop owners are as victimized as the customers. Big-time dealers make up fakes by the hundreds, then sell them one at a time to the shops, never too many in any one area."

"So poor little Anne-Louise probably doesn't know that her vase is phony."

"Right."

"That's good. She seems like a nice lady."

"Oh, she is. In fact, she took it quite personally when you and Judy left without buying the stone panther."

Tess visibly shivered.

"Hey, what is it with you and that statue?" he asked, remembering her reaction to the cat. She had actually backed away from it, as if it were some loathsome creature.

"I just thought it was ugly," she said offhandedly. Her manner wasn't convincing.

"But beauty is in the eye of the beholder, isn't it? And Judy liked it. Why didn't you let her buy it?"

"It's like I told her—that cat was not an appropriate present for an elderly maiden aunt." She took a sip of her drink and stared out the window, a pensive look on her face. "Probably would have frightened the old girl into a case of the vapors."

"Yeah, maybe you're right," he said thoughtfully. "It wouldn't look good sitting among pots of African violets and crocheted doilies. A statue like that would appeal more to a man, I guess."

"Mmm," she said, neither agreeing nor disagreeing. "As a matter of fact, I kind of liked it. Maybe I'll buy it myself."

"No." A definite look of panic flashed through her eyes, then was gone. "It's not a good buy. All that stuff about the palace of Versailles was nonsense. I've seen lots of statues like that—postwar junk from Japan."

He could tell she was lying. Why? he wondered.

"If you're really interested in acquiring an accent for your home," she continued, "I could help you pick out a quality piece, something that would be a good investment."

"But I don't want an investment," he argued, enjoying the spirited banter, wondering how far he could push her. "And I don't care how old it is. I like that cat. It would look good on my bookshelf."

"Believe me, you wouldn't like it once you got it home." Her voice had taken on that ominous quality that intrigued him and gave him the chills at the same time.

"What makes you so sure?"

The waiter chose that moment to deliver their sandwiches. Tess dug into hers, giving her something to do besides answer his question.

"You're superstitious, aren't you?"

When she looked up at him in surprise, he was pretty sure he'd hit the mark.

He pressed on. "You believe in omens and all that stuff. For some reason, you think the marble cat is bad luck."

"Yes, that's exactly it," she replied after a moment's hesitation. "A crouching cat is extremely bad luck. Why, my uncle once brought a figurine like that into his house, and—"

"Don't tell me. He got a splinter and they had to amputate his foot, right?"

She ripped a bite from her sandwich and chewed angrily, swallowed, then took a sip of her water. "You aren't taking this very seriously. Don't you believe me?"

"I believe you. I just don't believe in omens, or charms, or silly superstitions. Where did you learn about such nonsense? And why would an obviously enlightened, intelligent woman like yourself believe in them?"

"It's not nonsense," she said, shrilly enough that a woman from a neighboring table looked over curiously.

Nate decided he'd pushed Tess far enough. "Hey, let's not argue about it. I'm sorry. You have the right to believe whatever you want, and I shouldn't make fun of it. Truce?"

She nodded stiffly.

Her superstitions were probably a leftover habit from her unconventional childhood, he concluded. When he got to know her better, he would bring up this subject again and see if he could get a little closer to the truth.

❖ ———————— ❖

Tess actually enjoyed the afternoon, once they got off the subject of that awful statue. As they continued visiting antique shops, she found Nate to be a fascinating and funny companion. He didn't seem to be an expert on anything, so there were no long, boring dissertations on insurance underwriting or industrial pollution, but he knew a little something interesting about everything under the sun—apparently a by-product of his ten-year freelance-writing career.

"Yeah, I learned early on that if I was going to make a living as a writer, I could never turn down a money-making assignment, even if I knew nothing about the subject matter. Somehow or other, I always learn just enough to get by."

"So today the lesson is antiques?" she asked.

"That's right. I'll get a general feel for things now, and later, as I'm actually writing the story, I'll ask specific questions. Hey, how about this?" He pointed to a small, mahogany card table. "Twenty-five hundred bucks?" He examined the price tag. "Sheraton, Philadelphia, circa 1800."

"Hmm." Tess peered beneath the tabletop, pretending to look for a distinguishing mark. She laid her hand against the bare wood and took a deep breath. The swift impression she received was that of a white-haired man in knickers working on a hand lathe, lovingly tooling a length of mahogany that would become a table leg. As he worked he sang softly.

"Authentic as hell," she declared as she opened her

eyes. She found that Nate was standing behind her, looking over her shoulder. When she straightened, rather than backing away, he moved in closer, bringing their bodies into light contact. She was about to object when she realized he was only making room for a woman with a baby stroller to pass behind them.

She waited for the moment to pass, as she knew it would, but it seemed to last forever. Nate's nearness overwhelmed her.

"How can you tell it's real?" he asked softly, his breath fanning her hair.

How what was real? The table? "The, uh, wood grains. The way they're matched up, and the patina of the finish." All nonsense, but the best she could come up with.

At last he moved away. "Damn."

She took a deep breath and avoided his gaze, certain he would be able to read her wantonness in her eyes. She was actually aroused. She could feel the heat pooling in her abdomen.

With some effort, she brought her mind back to the subject at hand. Another authentic piece. That's the way it had gone all day. Every item Tess touched reeked of authenticity. Sometimes the vibrations were from former owners, but often she found that her energy tuned in to the actual manufacture of the object, and usually those images were positive, imbued with the artisan's creative spirit.

Hanging around a bunch of antiques hadn't been the ordeal she had expected. She wondered if that was because she was calling on her "gift" with a specific goal in mind. Although she'd had this ability for as long as she could remember, she'd never done much purposeful work with it. Most of the time she simply fought it, trying unsuccessfully to turn it off.

As they exited yet another shop Nate stopped and pointed up the street. "Hey, look where we ended up."

To Tess's discomfort, she discovered they had wandered right back to Anne-Louise's store.

"Let's go in and ask Anne-Louise where she got that vase," Nate said. "That should be a good lead."

"Oh, I don't think—"

"I won't tell her it's a fake, not until I have proof. Hey, what's wrong? You're all pale."

She wasn't surprised. Just the thought of going near that cat made her head spin.

"Oh, no, not the statue again." He sighed impatiently. "You don't even want to be in the same store with it?"

"No, I really don't," she said, knowing how ridiculous he must think her.

"You know, that's a pretty severe phobia you've got."

"It's not a phobia," she protested.

"Aversion, then. It's not so uncommon. I did a story once about phob—er, I mean, aversions, and you'd be surprised how many people have them. Did you know our former mayor is afraid of elevators? The editor of *Boston Life* can't go into a parking garage without breaking into a sweat. And my mother is terrified of moths." He laughed at that.

"It's not nice to laugh about such things," she told

him icily. "But I suppose you don't have any irrational fears."

"As a matter of fact, I do." He shoved his thumbs into the pockets of his jeans and looked around, reminding her of a little boy about to confess that he'd gotten into the cookie jar.

"Well, go on," she urged. "What are you afraid of?"

He shuddered. "Graveyards."

"Well, that at least makes sense. I'm not overly fond of them myself." They were filled with vibrations left by mourners, and sometimes with the darker residues of death itself. "A cemetery is a very sad place."

"Not sad, terrifying. I know that's not a rational, adult reaction, but there it is."

"And my reaction to the stone cat is just as illogical and just as real. You should be able to understand that."

He nodded, conceding the point. "Okay. Would you mind standing out here for a minute while I run in and ask Anne-Louise where she got the vase?"

That was a compromise she could live with, Tess supposed. "Okay. But promise me you won't look at the statue."

He winked. "Be back in a minute."

Tess paced the sidewalk outside the store. It hadn't escaped her attention that Nate hadn't promised. She wouldn't be surprised if he came out of that store with the Crimson Cat. It would be just like him to buy the damn thing to show her that it wasn't bad luck—for her own good, of course. To cure her of her so-called phobia.

Then again, maybe it was irresponsible of her to have left the cat statue where it was, to tempt innocent people like Judy and Nate. Maybe if she talked to Anne-Louise, the woman would tuck the figurine away somewhere where no one could find it. Of course, the longer Anne-Louise kept the statue, the more severe her own contact with the curse.

Tess was still trying to decide if she was ethically bound to act in Anne-Louise's behalf when Nate emerged from the shop less than five minutes later, empty-handed. She couldn't help breathing a sigh of relief that he hadn't bought the cat.

"Got it," he said triumphantly as they continued up the sidewalk. "Anne-Louise bought the vase from some slick dealer out of New York—even gave me his card. Oh, and you don't have to worry about the cat anymore. She sold it."

Tess stopped abruptly. "Sold it? When?"

"Just a couple of hours ago. I was thinking of buying it, just to prove to you—"

But Tess wasn't listening. She did an about-face and headed back to the shop.

"What the hell?" Nate demanded, two paces behind her.

She jerked open the door, sending the chimes into a frenzy, and walked straight up to Anne-Louise. "Who did you sell that cat statue to?"

Anne-Louise's welcoming smile faltered. "I don't know who bought it. I was taking a late lunch, and my assistant handled the sale."

Tess softened when she realized her abrupt manner

was offensive to the innocent shopkeeper, herself a victim of the cat's curse if that cast on her leg was any indication. "Is there a credit-card receipt?" she asked gently. "A check, maybe?"

The other woman's smile returned. "No, I believe the transaction was in cash. My assistant, Jenny, just left, but she'll be back on Monday if you want to ask her about it then. If one of her regular customers bought the statue, she'll know who."

"Yes, I'd like that." Tess fished in her bag for a card. "Would you have Jenny call me first thing Monday morning?"

"Of course, but why are you interested in who bought it?"

"I, uh . . ." Oh, dear. Now she'd have to tell another lie. Lying was getting to be a habit lately.

"She knew I liked it," Nate supplied, "and she wanted to buy it for me."

"Hmm, odd," Anne-Louise mused. "First no one wants it, now everyone does."

"Was there someone else inquiring?" Tess asked.

Anne-Louise nodded. "A man came in here not thirty minutes ago asking Jenny about the statue. I only heard bits and pieces of the conversation, but he claimed the cat was stolen from him, and he wants it back. He was most upset when he found out it had been sold."

What could that mean? Tess wondered frantically. Once someone had rid himself of the evil creature, why would he purposely seek it out again? She knew, from hearing family stories, that the statue was almost impossible to get rid of. And the curse, once it was visited upon you, remained with you forever. Damn, now she wished she'd paid more attention when Morganna had tried to teach her about this stuff.

"Did he tell you his name?" she asked.

"I believe it was . . . Tristan. Tristan Something. He was a swarthy gentleman, very, er, strange looking." Anne-Louise waited expectantly, perhaps hoping for some explanation from Tess. But Tess could think of nothing else to say. The man's name and description meant nothing to her.

"Are you ready to go?" Nate asked, sounding decidedly impatient.

"Yes, I'm done." She thanked Anne-Louise and they left. She noticed, as Nate held open the door, that he almost put his hand to her waist in a gentlemanly gesture, to guide her out of the store. Almost, but not quite.

She found herself almost aching for that incidental touch, which was exceedingly odd. She usually tried very hard to avoid touching. One of the things she had liked about Nate, one of the things that made her feel so comfortable with him, was that he kept his hands to himself.

Tess glanced at her watch. "I should be getting home," she said. "I don't like riding the T after dark by myself."

"After what happened last week, I don't like riding the T, period."

She gave him a mischievous grin. "Better watch

out. You'll be developing another phobia before you know it."

He waved away her concern as ridiculous. "I'll get over it. Anyway, on a day like today, why travel underground?"

"So you don't have to find a parking space," she quipped.

"I found one. Why don't you let me give you a ride home?"

The idea appealed to her in more ways than one. He'd been a perfect gentleman so far. She had no reason to believe his behavior would change if she got into a car with him.

"Okay," she said, realizing as she did so that she was reluctant to say good-bye to Nate. It was almost as if some invisible cord was now drawn between them, pulling insistently at her, urging her closer, closer.

He smiled broadly, showing her a flash of white teeth. "Great. I'm parked just . . ." He paused, and a frown creased his brow. "Wait. I forgot to tell you—I rode my Harley today. Is that okay?"

A motorcycle? Absolutely not! If she rode on the back of his bike, she would have to hold on to him . . . wrap her arms around him. And while the picture now forming in her mind was dangerously intriguing, that much physical contact could be disastrous. If he wasn't the type to guard his thoughts, she would probably know everything he was thinking.

Just now she didn't want to read his mind. What if he was thinking something vulgar about her? So many of the men she had touched, even casually, carried such lewd thoughts that it had turned her off completely. Even worse, she might discover that Nate wasn't in the least attracted to her.

"I'm a careful driver, really," he was saying. "And I have an extra helmet."

She shook her head vehemently. "I can't, I really can't. I'm sorry."

He nodded his understanding. "I'll accept that. And I won't even tease you about having a phobia."

"An aversion," she corrected him. "And a perfectly logical one. Everybody knows motorcycles are dangerous."

Again he nodded, appearing resigned. Then, unexpectedly, he grasped her hand. "There are a lot of antique stores in Boston. We could do this again."

She was so shocked that at first she couldn't answer. It wasn't the gesture that surprised her, or his invitation. It was the nonverbal communication that had knocked her speechless. From the moment of skin-to-skin contact, she had felt a rush of such friendly, unthreatening warmth and affection that for once in her life she didn't immediately try to tug her hand from another's grasp. She also felt the force of his desire, which commingled with her own.

"Tess?"

"Uh, yeah, I'm open," she finally managed, somewhat ungracefully, she thought, but her intelligent mind had gone all mushy.

She fairly floated home. This was the first time she had ever felt optimistic about her romantic prospects. If Nate Wagner could hold her hand and leave her feeling euphoric, maybe they could touch in other ways.

She could hardly wait to tell Judy. Judy, of course, had guessed all along that there was a spark between Tess and Nate. That was why she had tactfully disappeared this afternoon, claiming she had "pressing business to attend to." Now she would thoroughly enjoy telling Tess, "I told you so." And Tess wouldn't mind at all.

The phone was ringing as she walked through the front door. When she answered, she was delighted to find Judy on the other end of the line. "And you don't believe in karma," Tess scolded. "I was just getting ready to call—"

"Tess, hush and listen for a minute. I'm at Mass General."

Tess's heart skipped a beat, then thudded like a base drum. "What are you doing at the hospital? Is someone sick?"

"Yeah, me. Oh, God, Tess, I'm really sick and I'm scared out of my mind. Please, come stay with me until they find out what's wrong." Her voice, normally so brash and carefree, was choked with tears.

"Sit tight, I'm coming," was all Tess said before hanging up. Judy would understand that Tess would drop everything and get there as fast as she could.

As she pulled a denim jacket out of the closet, an awful thought occurred to her. It couldn't be the curse, could it? After all, Judy hadn't even touched the Crimson Cat, although she had expressed an interest in it.

No. Tess remembered clearly that a person actually

had to hold the statue, to be in possession of it—even temporarily, as Nate had been—in order for the powerful magic to take effect.

Anyway, this mysterious illness of Judy's was probably something minor—a sudden, violent onset of the flu, maybe, and she was overreacting. Judy never got sick. She probably didn't realize how miserable a simple case of the flu could feel.

Yes, that had to be it, Tess told herself firmly as she locked the door behind her. But she knew the awful sense of foreboding wouldn't leave her alone until she'd seen for herself that Judy was really all right.

THREE

Either Tess had disappeared, or she was deliberately avoiding him.

Nate had tried to reach her for two days. At the software company where she worked, her assistant informed him that Tess was "out of the office" for an indefinite period. When he called her home number, which he obtained easily enough from the phone book, all he got was her answering machine.

He had called that number several times for the pure pleasure of allowing her sweet, sexy answering-machine voice to wash over him, but he never left a message. It was a selfish thing, he supposed, but he didn't like being the one to wait around for the phone to ring. In case it didn't.

She couldn't be trying to avoid him, he decided. If she didn't want to talk to him, all she had to do was tell him, and she seemed intelligent enough to figure that out. Then where was she?

He wandered into the kitchen, popped the top on a beer, and considered what he might dig out of the freezer for dinner. He had at least a dozen rib-eye steaks in there, but he was sick of steak. Maybe he'd go out for seafood. He might as well live high while he could.

On the average he made a healthy income from his freelance writing, but the money was far from predictable. With his budgeting skills, or lack thereof, it was feast or famine—champagne and caviar one month, macaroni and cheese the next. Because he'd just received payment for copyediting a medical-school textbook, he'd splurged on rib-eye steaks.

Beer in hand, he returned to the living room and flopped onto his comfortably worn leather sofa, intending to make some notes on the fake-antiques story. Instead he gazed out the window on a dreary afternoon on Central Square. Then, in an almost automatic gesture, he picked up the cordless phone and dialed Tess's number again—from memory, this time.

"Hello?" came a breathless voice.

Nate was so surprised to have Tess in the flesh on the other end of the line that for a moment he said nothing.

"Listen, if you're the breather who's been calling, I've had just about enough of—"

"Whoa, wait a minute, I'm no breather. It's Nate Wagner. What's wrong? Is someone hassling you?" he asked sharply.

"Oh, hi, Nate." She sounded pleased to hear from him, but there was an unmistakable note of strain in her voice that put him on the alert. "And no, no one's hassling me, but I've had a bunch of hang-ups on my answering machine."

Nate gulped back an apology, unwilling to admit that at least some of those calls had been his. "How annoying," he said instead, silently promising the powers-that-be that next time he reached Tess's machine he would leave a message. "Where have you been, anyway?"

"How did you know I've been gone?" Suspicion tainted her words.

"Your assistant," he responded after he hoped wasn't a telltale pause. "When I couldn't get you at work, I tried your home number. You don't mind, do you?"

"No, I don't mind. What can I do for you?"

Her tone was smoothly professional, but again he noted the strain in her voice. He got the impression that she wanted to talk to him, but she had some urgent matter pressing on her mind. "Tess, what's wrong?" he asked gently.

She expelled an elaborate sigh. "It's Judy," she said, and then the story came tumbling out. "She's in the hospital. She got very weak on Saturday and went to the emergency room at Mass General. They think she has something called . . . God, I can't even remember. GBS, or something like that."

"Guillain-Barré syndrome?" Nate supplied as his stomach sank.

"Yes, that's it. You're familiar with it, then?"

"A little. I wrote a story about it a couple of years

ago. Is it . . . I mean, do they know if she'll be okay?"
He didn't remember a lot about the disease, only that it
produced paralysis in varying degrees. Some victims recovered fully. Many were left permanently disabled.
Some died.

"The doctors don't know yet. She's still on a down-
hill slide, though. She's getting weaker by the hour.
I've been spending a lot of time with her. Her parents
are retired in Texas, and she doesn't want to worry
them unless it's absolutely necessary. She's afraid
they'll fly up here in a panic. But her doctor told her
today she should notify her family—" Tess's voice
broke.

Her distress stabbed at his heart. "I'm sorry, Tess.
Is there anything I can do?" He made the offer sincerely, though he couldn't imagine being of any use in
such a situation. So he was surprised when she took
him up on his offer.

"Actually, there is something," she said slowly, as if
thinking out the solution to a taxing puzzle. "Judy's
doctor said the best thing for her right now is to keep
her spirits up and get her mind off her illness. Maybe
you could interview her—you know, ask her questions
about buying antiques. She does have some funny stories to tell."

"I'd be happy to, but do you really think that would
help?"

"Sure," Tess said, gaining enthusiasm. "You made
quite an impression on Judy. She thinks you're interesting. She would be very flattered by your attention,
and I know it would make her feel better."

Do you think I'm interesting? he wanted to ask. Selfish, selfish. "Okay. When should I go?"

"As soon as possible. Now, if you can. Frankly, I don't know how much longer she'll be able to talk. I can meet you at the hospital in an hour. Room three-thirty-two."

"Yeah, okay. It's that bad?"

"It's that bad," she confirmed. Now he could hear the tears that clogged her throat. Damn.

He was relieved Tess would be meeting him. The hospital wasn't his favorite place, not since he'd spent more than his share of time in one waiting room after another, and he didn't relish the idea of walking into Judy's room alone. Besides, Tess sounded as if she could use a shoulder to cry on.

Come off it, Wagner. His motives went beyond altruism, and far beyond professional interest. He was downright anxious to see her again, and to find out whether the spark of awareness that had flashed between them was real, or a figment of his hopeful imagination.

When Nate walked off the elevator on the third floor at Mass General, he immediately spotted Tess, looking rumpled but no less appealing in a belted sweater, a cotton print skirt, and gray ankle boots. She was watching for him, and she offered him a weary welcoming smile as she ran a nervous hand through her short hair.

His first instinct was to pull her into a protective hug, but something stopped him. He met her gaze, and in her eyes he saw so many emotions, he couldn't sort them out—longing, desperation, and fear. Definitely fear.

He still remembered that brief flash of panic he'd seen in her eyes when he had simply grasped her hand.

The need to feel her body next to his, if only briefly, almost overrode his common sense. He reached out to her. But instead of meeting him halfway, she grasped his hand in a clumsy greeting.

Nate's disappointment was almost tangible. He'd never had so much trouble reading a woman's signals before.

He squeezed her hand in return. "How's she doing?"

Tess shook her head. "Not good. I waited for you out here so I could warn you—she looks awful, with all those machines hooked up to her. But I told her you were coming, and she's looking forward to seeing you."

He nodded. "Let's do it, then." He reached into his jacket pocket for a notebook and pen, then followed Tess into the room.

Despite Tess's warning, Nate was shocked by Judy's appearance. She was hardly the same, vibrant woman who had argued with Tess over a cracked Chinese vase. Without her makeup and colorful clothes, she was a shadow of herself, gaunt and pale against the white sheets.

"Look who I found roaming the halls," Tess said brightly.

Before Judy could even respond with a greeting, Nate launched into his cheer-up-the-patient routine. It was one he knew well enough. "Hey, what's all this?"

he asked, making a dramatic sweep with his arm, taking in the various medical paraphernalia that stood like grim sentinels around Judy's bed. "Are you sick, or are you trying to make it into the *Guinness Book of Records* for 'Most Life-Support Equipment Attached to One Human Being'?"

Apparently it was exactly the right thing to say. Judy grinned up at him. "Maybe both. Will you promise to enter me posthumously if I croak?"

"You bet," he said as he pulled a chair up to the bed. "But only if you leave me something in your will." He noticed that Tess cringed slightly at the gallows humor. He couldn't blame her. But frank talk was sometimes a coping mechanism. "Now," he continued, "I understand you've had some interesting experiences buying antiques. But before we start, I want one thing understood. If you get tired of me, say the word and I'm outta here. Deal?"

Judy worked her arm out from under the covers and took his hand in a weak grasp. "Deal. Oh, Tess, honey, you must be sick of this room by now. I know I am. Why don't you take a break and go get yourself something to eat? Read a few pages of that romance novel hidden in your purse and relax for a few minutes. Nate and I will have a nice chat."

So, Tess read romance novels. Interesting. She appeared slightly reluctant to leave, but he urged her on out with a nod. Aside from the fact that Judy might need a break from her friend's well-meaning hovering, he wanted this chance to speak with her alone. If an opportunity presented itself, he might ask her about Moonbeam Majick.

Tess wandered down to the cafeteria, but the only thing she thought she could keep on her beleaguered stomach was a vanilla milkshake. She bought one, then returned to the third floor and paced in front of the nurses' station, wondering what Nate and Judy were talking about. She hoped Judy didn't have it in her head to play matchmaker.

These last three days had taken their toll on Tess. She had stayed by Judy's bedside day and night, unable to bear the thought of her friend lying in that sterile room, alone and afraid. But there was only so much Tess could take. By asking Nate to visit, she had been looking after her own concerns as well as her friend's. She needed a break. And she'd needed to see Nate Wagner again.

Tess had seen the silent understanding that passed between Nate and Judy, the grasp of hands. A warm, reassuring touch was one thing Tess couldn't provide. She was doubly glad now that she'd asked him to come, for Judy's sake as well as her own.

Nate spent what seemed like a long time in Judy's room, but when Tess checked her watch for the tenth time, only twenty minutes had passed.

"Did everything go okay?" she asked anxiously the moment he emerged into the corridor.

He nodded as he tucked his reporter's notebook into the inside pocket of his tweed jacket. "She gave me some great material and some good leads too. But I could tell she was getting tired. She wants to talk to you before she falls asleep."

"Okay. Nate, I can't thank you enough. You were great. Everyone else tiptoes and whispers around her, but you knew just what to say."

He shrugged. "My younger sister died of bone cancer a few years ago. She taught me how important humor is to someone who's sick."

"I'll try to remember that. Thanks again." She sensed that he wanted to give her a reassuring touch. Part of her longed for it. To feel his strong arms around her was something she'd dreamed of in unguarded moments. But her habitual caution held her back. She honestly didn't know what would happen if she let down her guard, and she wasn't prepared to deal with any surprises just now. She wanted to hang on to her fantasies about Nate a little longer, just a little.

She knew that eventually she'd have to let them go, but not now. She clutched her milkshake with both hands and stayed a safe distance from him. "Would you . . . would you wait here for a few minutes?" she asked, feeling shy. But she didn't want him to leave.

"I was planning to." He flashed a devilish smile, causing her heart to flutter at an alarming rate.

Before she could say or do anything silly, she nodded and ducked into Judy's room.

Judy was still smiling, though weakly. "Hey, that Nate is priceless. You better grab onto him fast."

"I'll do what I can," Tess said demurely, pushing

aside the disturbing imagery produced by the thought of grabbing on. "But I doubt he's interested."

"Oh, he's interested, all right."

"Why? What did he say? What did you say?"

Judy's expression became enigmatic. "Nothing important. Listen, I really did want to ask you a favor before I conk out again. Can you look in on Whiskers?"

Tess tried not to let her distaste show on her face. Cats, whether live or carved from marble, weren't her favorite animals, especially not Judy's cat. The overfed Whiskers wrapped his fat, furry, black body around Tess's ankles at every opportunity. Her mother used to tell her that witches inhabited the bodies of black cats. Tess suppressed a shiver.

"Sure, I can stop by your place and check on him," she forced herself to say, smiling all the while. "But I thought your neighbor Mrs. Glick was taking care of him."

"She is, but she called earlier and said Whiskers isn't eating. I want you to make sure he's okay. And, Tess, if anything happens to me—"

"Don't say that!" Tess cut in fiercely. "You're going to be fine."

"If anything happens to me," Judy persisted, "will you find a good home for Whiskers?"

"But nothing's going to—"

"Promise."

"Okay, I promise. But only if you stop talking nonsense."

"It's not nonsense. I might be dying, Tess, and you

better get used to the idea. Now go away. I want to sleep for a while." With that, she closed her eyes, indicating the subject wasn't open for discussion.

Rather than have Judy hear her snuffling, Tess left the room. She swiped at her tears with the back of her hand, embarrassed to have Nate see her crying. But as fast as she could wipe them away, new ones formed. Wonderful. Why did she have to pick now to cry?

"Judy asked me to go with you to feed the cat," he announced matter-of-factly. "She doesn't like to think of you riding the subway alone in the evening."

"I was planning to . . . go get . . . my car." Shaky sobs punctuated the sentence.

"I'll take you to Judy's," he said, brooking no argument. "And don't worry, I drove my car, not the Harley." As they passed the nurses' station on the way to the elevator, he grabbed a couple of tissues from a box on the desk and handed them to her wordlessly.

She was so grateful that he wasn't making a big deal of her tears that she would have agreed to anything he suggested.

The weather had taken a nasty turn, both cold and damp. Tess had accidentally left her jacket in Judy's room and didn't want to return for it, in case her friend was asleep. Nate, overcome with a ridiculous urge to be chivalrous, gave her his tweed blazer. She accepted it with a silent nod of gratitude, although it swallowed her whole. The hem hit her halfway to her knees, and the sleeves extended beyond her fingertips.

The oversized jacket, combined with her tears, should have made her look childlike. But Nate had no trouble remembering that Tess DeWitt was a hundred-percent full-grown woman. He could have offered her more warmth and comfort than a threadbare jacket, but he didn't intend to tread where he wasn't yet welcome. He settled for frequent covert glances at her as he drove toward Back Bay, drinking in the sight of her angel's face in profile, her damp, tear-shiny eyes, the rise and fall of her breasts, and she did nothing more provocative than breathe.

Patience was a virtue, he reminded himself.

When they reached Judy's fashionable Back Bay town house, for a moment all Nate could do was stare at the three-story Victorian brownstone. "Man, what did she do, rob a bank?"

But Tess wasn't listening. She was staring at a man wearing a dark overcoat who was walking down the sidewalk away from them.

"Tess?"

"That man," she said. "I think he was watching us."

"And I think your imagination is working overtime," Nate said, leading the way to the front porch.

Tess deactivated the burglar alarm and unlocked the door. "You're right. I haven't had much sleep the last three days. Still, that guy was kind of creepy looking."

They entered the luxurious town house and shook off the cold and damp. Someone, the neighbor, perhaps, had turned on the heat, but for some reason, Nate found the place far from cozy. In fact, Judy's home gave him a funny, unsettled feeling in the pit of his stomach. He wondered why.

"Here, kitty, kitty," Tess called softly as they went into the living room. The sofa and coffee table were strewn with shopping bags, probably from Saturday's outing. "Hmm, I wonder where the cat is? He knows I don't like him, so he's usually all over me like a rash the moment I walk through the door."

"Cats are perceptive creatures," Nate said. "He probably knows Judy is sick, and he's moping somewhere. My sister Cathy had a cat that was devoted to her. When she went into the hospital the first time, the cat disappeared. My dad and I looked everywhere. Yet the day we brought Cathy home, there was the cat on the front porch, waiting for us."

"What did it do when your sister died?" Tess asked gently.

"Disappeared again. We never found it."

Tess shivered. "That's why I don't like cats. They're spooky. Here, kitty, kitty," she tried again, halfheartedly.

Nate set off to search for the cat. There was no sign of it downstairs or on the second floor. But on the third floor, when he entered one of the bedrooms, he heard a low, fearful growl.

He got on his hands and knees and peered under the bed. There he found a huge ball of black fur scrunched back in a corner. Two round, orange eyes glowed menacingly from the fur ball, which hissed when Nate extended a hand toward it.

"C'mon, cat," he cajoled. "Tess is going to feed you some nice, smelly canned food."

The cat hissed again.

"Come on, now. Judy has enough to worry about without you going on a hunger strike." He reached closer, intending to pet the cat. In a lightning-quick move, Whiskers made a sweeping slash with one paw, delivering a wicked scratch to Nate's forearm.

"Ouch!" He quickly withdrew his arm and clamped his other hand over the scratch to stanch the flow of blood. "Damn cat! Starve, then." He turned to find Tess standing in the doorway, holding a bowl of cat food, her blue eyes big as saucers.

"You found Whiskers, I see."

"Unfortunately." He didn't want her to see the blood, but since it was seeping out from under his hand, he didn't have much choice. "I better wash this out before I bleed all over Judy's floor."

Tess grimaced as she set the bowl just inside the doorway, where Whiskers couldn't miss it. "This way. I know Judy has some first-aid stuff in her bathroom on the second floor."

He followed Tess down the stairs, his senses still sharp enough to appreciate the graceful sway of her hips. It would take more than a cat's scratch to distract him from his growing attraction to her. Even the story about Moonbeam Majick had taken a backseat. He hadn't asked Judy about her friend's alter ego, for fear of setting off a reaction that would drive Tess away from him before they'd even had a chance.

Judy's master-bedroom suite was furnished with

fussy, feminine French Provincial furniture—authentic, if Nate had learned anything about antiques. He thought the decor was cloyingly sweet.

The master bath, however, was a different story. Now, *this* he could get used to. Big enough to fly an airplane through, the bathroom boasted pale peach-colored fixtures against snow-white tile, and frothy, monogrammed towels with peach-and-white stripes. The square tub, plenty big enough for two, particularly appealed to him.

Nate had never bathed with a woman before. The small, footed tub in his Cambridge apartment, where he had lived for the past seven years, was barely big enough to accommodate his tall frame, much less a guest. He glanced at the tub and then at Tess, and he couldn't help the slow smile that spread across his face.

Fortunately she was too concerned with his minor injury to notice. She turned on the faucet at the sink, and a stream of warm water issued from a gold swan's neck. "Here, wash out that scratch with soap and water," she said in a no-nonsense tone. "I'll see what I can find in the way of antiseptic."

Ick. He hated first aid. The treatment always seemed worse than the original injury. But he dutifully washed out the cut, inhaling sharply at the sting of soap. Then he watched with some trepidation as Tess rummaged around inside a cabinet, pulling out various bottles and boxes and tubes.

"Is your arm still bleeding?" she asked.

"Nah, it's slowing down." He shut off the water and blotted his arm with a wad of tissue.

She handed him a bottle. "Spray it down good with this stuff to kill the germs."

He did as directed, biting his lip to keep from yelping. "Ouch. What are you trying to do, kill me?"

"Now spread some of this antibiotic stuff around," she said, ignoring his complaint.

"You're really paranoid about infections, aren't you?"

"You would be, too, if you'd known my uncle. Let's see, where's the adhesive tape?"

Great. He looked forward to having adhesive tape stuck to the hair on his arm. When she turned back around, her hands full of gauze pads and tape, he couldn't miss the hesitation in her eyes.

"I guess I'll have to put these bandages on for you."

"Yup. I can't do it one-handed. Why are you afraid to touch me?" he asked, amused but curious. "I won't bite." Not unless she wanted him to.

"I'm not afraid," she retorted quickly. As if to prove that she wasn't, she resolutely grasped his hand and stretched his arm out in front of her, placed two gauze pads along the cut, and taped them into place. Her touch was crisp and clinical, very businesslike, yet comforting, as if she'd wrapped his whole body in velvet. He enjoyed it a lot more than he should have.

Maybe first aid wasn't so bad after all.

Tess, however, didn't seem to be enjoying herself at all. As she worked she bit down on the inside of her cheek. Her breathing came in short, quiet gasps, and a thin sheen of moisture broke out on her upper lip.

Maybe the blood bothered her. He remembered

how pale she'd turned at Anne-Louise's when he'd pricked his finger.

"Are you okay?" he asked.

She fastened the last strip of tape, then quickly pulled her hands away and wiped her damp palms on a towel. "Fine. I'm sorry I dragged you into this. That scratch must hurt like hell." She turned and began stuffing the medical supplies back into the cabinet.

"It's better now, thanks." He thought the elaborate bandage was overkill, but after all the trouble she'd gone to, he didn't dare criticize.

She closed the cabinet door and turned to face him. "I guess we've done about all we can do for Whiskers," she said.

"All I'm willing to do, at any rate. Even if he doesn't eat for a week, he's in no danger of wasting away. The cat must weigh twenty pounds."

"At least." She wrinkled her nose in distaste.

Tess edged past Nate and out the door, apparently anxious to be away from the intimate confines of the luxurious bathroom. What he would give to spend some time in there with her under different circumstances.

"If you can spare a few more minutes, I'd like to stay and straighten up the place," she said as they made their way downstairs. "When Judy comes home from the hospital, she won't be in any mood to clean house."

"I'm not in any hurry," he said. "I'll start on the kitchen, if you'll handle all those shopping bags in the living room."

"Oh, you don't have to help. You shouldn't do anything," she said as they paused by the kitchen door. "Your arm—"

"Doesn't hurt at all," he said with bravado. It throbbed like a sore tooth. The minute he got home, he was going to pop some aspirin and wallow in his pain. "I'll load the dishwasher. I can do that one-handed."

She hesitated, then reluctantly nodded and left him to perform his chosen chore.

He actually didn't mind domestic work. Having been a bachelor for umpteen years, he had mastered the basics and performed them often enough that at least he wasn't embarrassed to bring home a guest, whether it be his great-aunt Edna or a lover. His apartment probably wouldn't pass the white-glove test, and the clutter occasionally got out of control, but at least he didn't have marauding herds of dust bunnies loping around.

He whistled tunelessly as he rinsed off a beautiful, paper-thin china plate. It looked like a piece from an heirloom set—Judy's mother's wedding china, perhaps. Judy was one of the few people he'd ever met who actually ate off her china.

He was about to set the plate in the dishwasher when a shrill scream pierced the domestic quiet. The plate slipped from his grasp and fell with a crash to the tile floor. Without missing a beat, he bolted from the kitchen through the dining room and into the living room, where Tess stood frozen in place, her frightened gaze fixed on something he couldn't see at floor level.

"What is it? A mouse?"

"Come see for yourself," she said in a shaky voice.

He inched past her and peered around the coffee table. There, still half-hidden by the paper bag and tissue paper in which it had been wrapped, was the red marble cat, its yellow eyes glittering malevolently.

Tess grabbed his elbow and pulled him away before he got too close. "Now do you believe in omens?"

FOUR

Every muscle in Tess's body felt paralyzed as she stared at the red stone cat peeking from its brown paper covering. What to do? She didn't want to touch it, but it seemed imperative that she remove it from Judy's house.

"That—that can't be what made Judy sick," Nate said, sounding like the soul of reason. "It's ridiculous. There's no such thing as a—a bad-luck charm, or whatever the hell you think this thing is."

Finally Tess managed to tear her gaze away from the statue and look at Nate. Despite his eminently sane words, there was a certain wildness in his eyes, and his chest rose and fell with his unnaturally rapid respiration. She knew he was trying to be logical, but some part of him was plenty spooked by the appearance of the statue.

"Maybe we should get out of here," he suggested in a calmer voice.

Tess took a deep breath, trying to settle her own runaway nerves. "Okay. But we're taking the cat with us. We'll steal it."

"Why don't we buy it instead?" Nate said, reaching for his wallet. Tess couldn't tell if he was making fun of her or humoring her, or if maybe he was entertaining the possibility that she was right about the curse. "That way, ownership will pass to us."

"Good idea. Where'd I leave my purse?"

"I'll buy it," he said decisively, throwing fifty bucks onto the coffee table. "I'm the one who doesn't believe in curses. Maybe it's like voodoo. You have to believe in it before it can harm you."

"You didn't believe in it—or even know about it—when you got pushed in front of the subway train."

"That was a coincidence. C'mon, let's go. You left your purse in the entry hall." He gingerly picked up the cat. Tess noticed that he kept the paper sack wrapped around the creature so that he didn't actually touch it.

So, he didn't believe in bad luck, huh? Maybe not, but he wasn't taking any unnecessary chances.

Tess locked Judy's front door as Nate hovered protectively behind her. She appreciated his concern, but she wished he'd go on ahead with that nasty animal. She could literally feel her skin crawl when she was close to it. Her scalp prickled. Every hair stood on end.

She dropped Judy's key into her purse and turned. That's when she saw the man again, the dark one who'd been loitering on the sidewalk when they'd arrived. She gave an involuntary gasp and, without even thinking about it, laid a restraining hand on Nate's arm. Immediately, vibrations from the cat traveled through Nate's body, through his clothes, and up her arm to settle like a cold shroud around her heart. She jerked her hand back as if she'd been burned.

"What is it?" Nate asked.

Tess gathered her wits. "That man. He was here when we arrived, just hanging around. He gives me the creeps."

"He's probably just waiting for a bus or something."

"Buses don't come down this street, and this isn't the sort of neighborhood where people loiter."

"Well, what are we supposed to do? He's not exactly committing a crime."

Nate was right, of course. She was getting paranoid. But she kept remembering what Anne-Louise had said about a swarthy man wanting to buy the cat.

"Just keep an eye on him," Tess said in a low voice. "He might be a mugger. Don't let him take us by surprise."

"Shoot, why not?" Nate muttered as they scurried down the sidewalk toward his car. "Maybe we'll luck out and *he'll* steal the cat."

The man didn't seem to be paying them a lot of attention, but neither did he stroll away. Tess watched him warily from the corner of her eye while Nate chucked the Crimson Cat into the trunk of his beautifully restored Ford Fairlane. She felt better once the thing was out of sight.

She also felt better once she was safely inside Nate's

car with the doors locked and his big, reassuring body next to hers. She even felt an alien urge to scoot across the old-fashioned bench seat and sit next to him. She'd spent her whole life edging away from people, hoping she wouldn't have to make an excuse for why she didn't want to hold hands or hug or cuddle. She didn't know quite how to handle this weird compulsion of hers to share Nate's space.

Before he put the car in gear, he glanced over at her, invitation in his eyes. "It's warmer next to me."

She looked down. "I know. I just . . ."

"Are you involved with someone else?" he blurted out.

"No! It's nothing like that."

"A bad experience with a man?" he asked more gently.

She wanted to crawl under the seat and avoid his probing gaze. "I have reasons for acting the way I do. You wouldn't understand."

"Try me. Is it just a general distrust of the male sex? I'd feel better knowing it's not personal."

Dammit, why did he have to be so endearing? All right. If he wanted to hear the truth, she'd give it to him. "If I touch you, I'll be able to read your mind. Everything you're thinking."

Nate didn't reply for a few moments. Instead he put the car in gear and pulled away from the curb. Then he chuckled. "That's a frightening thought."

He didn't believe her, of course. But at least she'd defused his question. Any more cajoling, and she'd have given in, scooting across the seat to tuck up against him. Instead she fastened her seat belt.

They'd gone less than ten blocks, neither of them saying anything, when Tess heard a *whump* and a *flap-flap-flap* as the car listed to the right.

"Aw, hell," Nate said. "A flat."

Tess put her head in her hands. In one respect, she was relieved the curse had apparently followed them. Maybe the pressure would be off Judy now. In another . . . she and/or Nate was in the grip of a curse! She'd never been cursed before. For the first time in a long time she wished for Morganna's guidance. Her mother was so learned in so many areas, including everything arcane or occult. But all of that knowledge was locked inside a brain that was no longer fully functional.

"Hey, Tess, you don't think that statue is responsible for this, do you? 'Cause I'm here to tell you, my tires needed replacing a couple of months ago and I didn't do it. It's one of those things I put off even though I knew I shouldn't. *That's* why we got a flat."

"I know," she said, trying to sound convinced. "I'm sure you're right. I'm just a little jumpy." That was an understatement. "You do have a spare, don't you?"

"Yeah. I'm not *that* foolhardy."

"Then can I help you change the tire?" Keeping busy might prevent her from dwelling on unpleasant possibilities. "You're injured."

"You just stay warm inside the car. I'll have the job done in a few minutes." He got out and slammed the door.

Despite his assurance that he had everything under control, Tess got out too. The weather had turned distinctly unpleasant, cold and misty with a biting wind. Even wearing Nate's jacket, she had to wrap her arms around herself and clamp her jaw firmly shut to keep her teeth from chattering.

Nate, seemingly oblivious to the cold in his shirt-sleeves, had to open the trunk to get the tire and the jack. Tess averted her eyes.

Nate noticed, but he didn't say anything.

I don't believe in luck, good or bad, Nate told himself as he set about the task of changing the tire. All this was a giant coincidence. But he had to admit, discovering the statue in Judy's apartment had made his heart jump into his throat.

One thing was for sure: Tess believed with all her heart that the statue really was evil, that it caused bad luck. The fear in her lovely blue eyes was too real to be an affectation. He didn't believe it was a simple superstition, either. Her fear went deeper than that. There was something personal in her aversion to the stone cat.

She'd seen it before their encounter in the antique shop.

Whatever the story, he intended to find out more about it. Who knew, perhaps it tied in with Tess's Moonbeam Majick history. Might make an interesting sidelight to his story.

It seemed to take him forever to change the tire.

The jack was balky. Every single lug nut was a challenge, as if they'd all been welded on. The spare was low, too, though it would probably make it to a service station.

Since Tess hovered nearby during the entire ritual, he asked her to hold the lug nuts. He couldn't help but notice that when he asked for them back, she dropped them one at a time into his hand rather than risk touching him.

When she handed him the last lug nut, he made a point of brushing her hand with his. Was it his imagination, or had he actually seen a spark flare between their two hands in the darkness? He heard her sharp intake of breath.

"Keep your mind on business," he murmured to himself.

"What?" Tess said.

"All finished." He gave the last nut one final twist with the lug wrench. The wrench slipped, and he banged his hand against the rough road surface, scraping his knuckles raw. In deference to Tess, the string of curses that spouted from his mouth were only mildly obscene.

"Oh, are you okay?"

"I'll live." He stuck his injured hand under his arm and squeezed his eyes closed until the pain subsided a bit. How many tires had he changed in his life? he wondered. And he'd never hurt himself before.

Hell, the damn panther statue was giving *him* the willies.

Since Tess still seemed to want to help, he let her

ratchet the jack down while he wrestled the flat tire into the trunk. In a couple of minutes they were back on the road. They stopped at the first service station they came to for a shot of air into the spare, then continued on their way.

"My place is a lot closer than yours," he said as casually as he dared. "It's been a long, miserable day, and I've got a good bottle of brandy tucked away for just such an occasion. What do you say we stop there and warm up a little before I take you back to your place?"

"I really need to go home," she said. Her voice held just enough hesitation that he persisted.

"But what about the cat?" He knew she would feel guilty sticking him with it. "Maybe we should stop at the nearest bridge and drop it off."

Tess shook her head. "Won't work. It's been tried." She glanced over quickly at him to see if he'd caught the significance of her revelation.

He had. "You know this cat, then? You don't just hate cats in general?"

She sighed. "Can't you just take me home?"

He had her now. "*I'm* the one who plunked down fifty bucks for the cat and lobbed it into my trunk. It's mine now. The least you could do is tell me about it. Explain what I'm up against."

Again she sighed. "Okay. Did you say something about brandy?"

He suppressed a smile of satisfaction. Once he got Tess going about this bad-luck statue, the conversation would naturally segue into her past as Moonbeam. Perfect.

He felt only a small stab of guilt at manipulating her with this superstition nonsense. Maybe when all was said and done, he would do her a favor by convincing her that superstitions weren't legitimate. After all, it couldn't be much fun to live with this kind of fear all the time.

Nate lucked out and found a parking spot within half a block of his apartment house. After he and Tess had gotten out of the car and he'd locked the doors, he headed for the trunk.

"No!" Tess cried. "Leave it where it is. For God's sake, don't bring the thing into your home."

"Okay, maybe you're right," he said. "The less we handle it, the better. Right?"

"I would think so."

Nate was more and more intrigued. He couldn't wait to get her talking.

As he unlocked his front door at the top of the stairs, he felt a sudden reluctance to allow Tess inside. He was such a . . . bachelor. Earlier, at Judy's place, he'd been congratulating himself for knowing how to load a dishwasher. But how long had it been since he'd tidied up his own place? A couple of weeks?

With a shrug he ushered her inside and flipped on a light. Could be worse, he decided. A couple of empty pizza boxes, a beer can or two, some unopened junk mail, and wilted plants. Besides that, everything was basically clean. He sat Tess down on his pride-and-joy leather sofa, but before her rear even made contact with the cushions, she wiggled sideways and landed in one of his two tweed club chairs instead.

"The sofa's more comfortable," he said.

"Not for me."

He puzzled over her explanation, but she didn't elaborate. So he shrugged and launched a whirlwind cleaning tour of the living room, the leavings of which he thrust down his garbage chute. Then he grabbed two glasses from the kitchen along with the unopened bottle of cognac.

He found Tess sitting exactly where he'd left her, perched nervously on the edge of the club chair, hands clenched, eyes darting around.

"You look like you could use a snort of this," Nate said, sitting on the sofa, wishing he could have finagled a way to sit beside her. He poured a generous measure of the amber liquid into each snifter, then handed her one.

"I think we should drink to Judy's swift recovery," he said, sincerely meaning it. As little time as he'd spent with Judy, he genuinely liked her. And he could tell that Tess loved her like a sister.

She nodded and flashed the beginnings of a brave smile. "Yes, that's an excellent idea." They clinked their glasses, then each took a sip. "Mmm," Tess said after swallowing. "Burns all the way down. Good."

"It'll warm you all the way to your toenails too."

After his second sip of brandy, he set the snifter on his mahogany coffee table. That's when he noticed one of his reporter's notebooks, sitting on the table inches from Tess's right knee. Aw, hell. All his notes about

Moonbeam Majick were in there. If she should stumble onto that information, she would know that he'd engineered their supposedly random meeting at the antique shop. She would know why he was pursuing her, why he was so curious about her, and she wouldn't be happy about it.

Although he had to admit, his curiosity extended far beyond journalistic instincts at this point. Part of him, that small part that was still innocent and believed in fairy tales, wished he'd never offered to write this story. It wished he'd really been shopping for a doll for his older sister and had chanced a meeting with a pretty blonde he'd known nothing about except that he liked her figure and her smile and the hypnotic sound of her voice.

That tiny, irrational part of him was wishing like crazy he had a chance in hell of getting her to forget all this curse nonsense and go out to a movie with him.

Yeah, right. He would be lucky if she didn't throw his brandy in his face and abandon him to his fate with that damn cat.

Still, if he snatched the notebook away now, she would be suspicious. He would simply not leave her alone with it again. He would sit there, guarding it like a German shepherd, till it was time to take her home.

"So," he said when she sat back in her chair, looking as if maybe the brandy was taking effect. "Tell me the whole story about this wretched statue."

"You won't believe it," she said flatly. "You'll just think I'm a total basket case."

"Try me."

If anything, she seemed even more reluctant. "Look, the brandy is nice and everything, but why don't I just call a cab—"

"Try me," he said again. "I can't guarantee I'll believe you a hundred percent, but I promise not to laugh at you. And I'll take you home as soon as you're done."

"Promise? It'll sound pretty outlandish to you."

He nodded. "Start at the beginning."

"Well, okay. See, no one knows exactly where the cat came from originally, but it's really old. Back in the 1800s, there was this Gypsy woman who lived in the woods near a town in Connecticut. The townspeople didn't have a doctor, or a priest, so they relied on the Gypsy for lots of things—cures for illnesses, blessings, good-luck charms, and some charms that weren't so nice. The Gypsy had a thriving business, until my great-grandmother—her name was Lass— moved to town. She was a . . ." Tess searched for the word.

A witch? Nate was burning to ask. He'd read in his research materials that Morganna, Tess's mother, claimed to come from a long line of witches.

"I guess in today's society she would be called a healer or an herbalist, something like that. She offered herbal remedies and, um, blessings, and unlike the Gypsy, she didn't charge money for her services. You can imagine what this did to the Gypsy's business."

Nate nodded.

"Only the people who wanted evil stuff—curses on their enemies, that kind of thing—continued to see the Gypsy because Lass wouldn't touch black magic."

Tess leaned back in her chair, relaxing slightly. "Well, the Gypsy finally decided she'd had enough. She came to Lass's house with a gift, a supposed peace offering."

"The cat statue."

"Right. But she'd put a powerful curse on it, a curse that affected not only great-grandmother, but all of her descendants and, apparently, anybody who came into possession of the statue. It's called the Crimson Cat, by the way."

"Uh-huh."

She set her glass down on the table with a thunk. "See? I knew you wouldn't believe any of this. You think I'm a nutcase."

"No, not at all. You're merely recounting a bit of family legend. Nothing nutty about that."

"Unless I believe it. Which I do. My great-grandmother sickened and died within months of receiving the statue—that was after her herb garden shriveled and her goats' milk soured. Then my grandmother inherited the statue. She went through four husbands, each dying more tragically than the last until finally Grandma killed herself."

Nate shivered despite himself. "That's awful."

"Tell me about it."

"Then did your mother inherit?"

"No, not yet. My uncle got it."

"Not the one who got the cut and lost his—"

"The very same. By this time the curse was well-known, so he decided to sell the statue. The collector who bought it died in a car accident on his way home.

The lawyer who handled his estate found the bill of sale for the cat in the man's effects, and since the estate was in debt, he returned the statue and got his money back. Then my uncle tried to throw the thing off a bridge."

"And what happened?" Nate asked, fascinated despite himself. True or not, it was a pretty good story she was weaving.

"A little boy from the village found the statue, undamaged, and dragged it up from the riverbed. His mother took one look at it, recognized it as belonging to my uncle, and back to my uncle the statue came. The little boy, incidentally, caught meningitis two weeks later and died."

"This is really interesting, Tess, but you'll forgive me for asking this. How do you know this story is true?"

"As a reporter, you're obligated to ask, I guess," she said. Nate was relieved that she didn't seem to be insulted. "I heard the early part from a great-aunt. My uncle told me his part himself, shortly before he was killed in a plane crash. That was *after* the business with the splinter and gangrene, I might add. The rest I experienced personally."

"I assume your mother got the statue next."

Tess nodded. "It happened when I was ten. Before that, she was much the same as my great-grandmother was—an herbalist, a natural healer. Most of the women on that side of the family were interested in the healing arts and the arcane. Mother read auras and collected crystals and meditated twice a day. But as soon as the statue arrived at our house, something sinister started happening to her. She turned to a darker sort of magic."

Yes! This was the stuff Nate had been waiting for.

Tess got fidgety again. She picked up her brandy snifter, then set it down without taking a sip. She fiddled with some coasters, then with a brass candlestick.

Nate's heart rose into his throat when she absently touched his notebook. Whoa, he told himself when he was ready to lunge across the table and grab the notebook from her. She hadn't opened it yet.

All at once a strange light came into her eyes. She frowned as her gaze became unfocused. Then she flashed him an angry scowl, and he could have sworn he saw blue sparks coming from her eyes.

She threw the notebook onto the table. "You son of a bitch!"

"What? Excuse me?" What had he done?

"You're using me. I trusted you. I was pouring my heart out to you, and the whole time all you want is to write a story about me. It was all a lie—all of it!"

FIVE

Tess had to get out of there. She rarely got angry, but when she did, her temper could boil over into rage, and Lord help whoever was in her path. She didn't trust herself to be logical or reasonable until the anger had run itself out; the best course of action was to get away from Nate and reclaim her precious solitude till she felt in control again.

"How did you know that?" Nate asked, sounding more bewildered than defensive. "How did you know I was planning to write a story about you?"

She narrowed her blue eyes and held up her hands in a classic spell-casting pose, like the Wicked Witch of the West. "My boogie-woogie witchy powers, how else? Now, if you'll excuse me, I'm going to catch a cab home. I have to feed my black cat and brew up some eye-of-newt tea!" She grabbed her purse and headed for the door.

Nate was right behind her. "Wait, you can't go!"

"Why not?" She jerked the door open and stepped onto the landing.

"You're going to leave me alone with a cursed cat statue in my trunk?"

That gave her pause. Much as she wanted to see the last of Nate Wagner, she *had* gotten him involved in the cat thing. The beast was still in his trunk, and he didn't take the threat seriously. What if something happened to him, something worse than a scratch or an uncomfortable brush with a subway?

Okay. If she were honest, she would have to admit that she really didn't want to see the last of him, either. He was a most intriguing man, the first ever to touch her without making her skin crawl.

She folded her arms and looked at him mutinously. No sense in letting him off easy. "You lied to me."

He conceded with a nod. "If I'd come right up to you and asked to write a story about Moonbeam Majick, what would you have said?"

"I'd have run as far and as fast as I could."

"I figured that. I thought if you could get to know me first, trust me a little bit, then I could ease into the subject of your past."

"And if I still was against it?" When he didn't respond right away, Tess discovered she was waiting breathlessly for his answer.

Finally he said, "I don't honestly know. I'd like to believe I would have honored your wishes. I can be a hard-ass sometimes, but I'm not ruthless."

Did she dare believe him? Or was this just another cramping of the truth to manipulate her? Then it occurred to her that she didn't have to guess. She had a foolproof method of discovering his true intentions, even if he didn't know the truth himself. "Give me your hand."

"Huh?"

"Just let me hold your hand for a moment."

"Okay." He held out one hand, palm up, as if he expected her to read his fortune in the lines and creases there. Instead, she took his hand in both of hers, lightly touching it. She closed her eyes.

Damn. He was so sincere, it was astounding. He had no intention of doing anything that would harm her.

"What are you doing?" he asked suspiciously.

"Shh." There it was again, that flash she'd experienced earlier, but it was stronger this time. Skin against skin, breathing, scents commingled, the hot touch of fevered fingers, questing, murmured lovers' words—

"What?" he asked more insistently this time.

She gasped and dropped his hand as if it were a burning coal. Holy moth-eaten cod. The images were stronger now, more distinct, too real to be dismissed as the frustrated yearnings of an overripe virgin. She and Nate were on a path toward intimacy, and their destiny was hurtling toward them at an alarming rate. Time was a fluid thing within the psychic world she knew, but she'd learned to guess.

A week, no more.

Destiny wasn't quite the right word, though, because free choice was always an option. Shadows of the future weren't carved in stone. Paths could be altered, the future could be changed.

"Tess! Are you okay?"

She realized she'd been staring at a blank wall, trancelike, for interminable seconds. Now she looked at Nate. The concern on his face, in the depths of those velvety brown eyes, was very real.

"I'm fine."

"You're zoning out on me, and I know you didn't have that much brandy."

"I was just thinking about something." She cleared her throat, trying to bring herself back to full, here-and-now consciousness. "I should go home. Just promise me you won't do anything with the statue until you talk to me."

"Huh, don't worry. I'm not going to touch it. Um, *will* you talk to me?"

"Yeah," she answered, her reluctance somewhat feigned. She didn't want to say good-bye forever. There was too much there to walk away from. "You're right, I can't stick you with the cat. I'll help you get rid of it."

"Let me get my car keys." He started to duck back inside his apartment.

"No! I'm not riding around the streets of Boston with that *thing* in your trunk. I'll take a cab."

"Okay, okay. I'll walk you down a few blocks to Cambridge Square. There's always a cab hanging around there."

She nodded.

Nate stepped inside his apartment to grab a jacket

off his coatrack—a leather bomber instead of his tweed blazer. Then he and Tess emerged from the building into the night. The wind had died down, but it was colder, and a malevolent mist hovered around the streetlights.

Tess shoved her hands into her skirt pockets and hunched against the harsh environment.

"Jeez, I forgot you don't have a jacket," he said. "Take mine. He started to remove the bomber, but she shook her head. Besides the fact that it was leather— cows didn't die pleasantly, she'd discovered long ago— it was also intimately Nate. She'd had enough of that for one evening. Her body still tingled from holding his hand.

They walked to the corner, and when no cabs were apparent, Nate found a store with a front stoop they could sit on. A cab would be along shortly, he assured her.

"So," he said, "do you really think a story about your past would be terrible?"

"Are you kidding? It would do my career irreparable harm. I'm a software developer with a conservative company. What do you think would happen to my reputation if people found out I was—that I used to be— that people once thought I was a witch? That I was called Moonbeam?"

"You were only a child."

"A seriously disturbed child in a radically dysfunctional home who underwent years of therapy. That kind of mark on one's past doesn't go away. Even in this enlightened age, people aren't tolerant of mental aberrations. I do not want my past bandied about as fodder for anyone's entertainment."

He said nothing for a while. Then, abruptly, he changed the subject. "What were you doing with my hand?"

"Witchy stuff," she said flippantly.

"No, really."

"That's what you'd call it. Let's just say I have a highly developed form of woman's intuition."

"You were touching my hand the way you touched those antiques the other day," he pressed. "And you got that same look on your face."

She'd revealed enough of herself for one day, particularly if Nate was ready to rush home and type up her answers into a story she didn't want written. "There's a cab." She rose from the steps, intending to step to the curb and wave the cab down. Suddenly a dark, solid form stepped in front of her.

Her breath caught in her throat. It was him, the swarthy man from Judy's neighborhood. "Excuse me, miss."

"I have to catch my—"

He grabbed her arm when she attempted to dart around him. "Please, I must speak to you."

Dark, repugnant images assaulted her brain. Stifling, suffocating, evil . . . She jerked her arm away.

"Hey!" Nate objected.

"You have something I want," the man said, his voice low, menacing. "Let's speak reasonably about it."

"Not a chance, Mac." Nate put a protective arm around Tess's shoulders. "C'mon, Tess."

The man grabbed at her again. This time she didn't attempt to pull away. A six-inch knife glittered in his other hand.

Nate froze, too, though he muttered a resigned, "Ah, hell."

"No!" Tess shouted. She knew what he wanted. She also knew, with some inner wisdom, that to give him the statue would invite an even worse tragedy than had already befallen them.

The man brought his knife closer to Tess's face. "Shut up. You're only a child. What do you know?"

Then Nate, easygoing, friendly Nate, got a look on his face that Tess had never seen before, a nearly palpable fury that rolled off of him in waves. His entire body tensed, then he leaned back slightly. One of his feet shot out in a blur of motion to connect with the other man's midsection.

In a tenth of a second the man was doubled over, groaning.

"Run!" Nate ordered, taking Tess's hand in case she had it in her head to ignore his advice.

She didn't. She took off running with him. They ducked into an alley, their legs pumping in unison. It was too dark for Tess to see much, but Nate led her on an unerring path around discarded boxes, garbage cans, and Dumpsters. Then it was through a small parking lot, over a low fence, and all at once they were in back of Nate's building again.

"Is . . . he . . . following?" she asked, gasping for breath.

"I don't think so."

"What did you do to him?"

"What, you mean that kick?" He shrugged. "Tai kwon do. Haven't practiced it in a while, but I guess I still got it." He led her through the back door of his building, swaggering only a little.

"Whatever it was, thank you. You might've just saved my life." The memory of that knife poised inches from her face, her throat, gave her chills.

"Yeah, well, next time give him the purse, all right?"

"The purse?" Tess trooped after him up the stairs, her familiar little vinyl purse clutched against her. She knew she was supposed to be on her way home, but all she could think about was the cozy security of Nate's apartment and the warmth of that brandy hitting her stomach. "He didn't want my purse. He wanted the Crimson Cat."

"Huh? He didn't say that. He said you had something he wanted."

"Nate, didn't you recognize him? He's the man who was hanging around outside Judy's town house."

"I don't . . . I mean, I don't think so. It was dark. How could you tell?"

"I just could. He wants that statue, and apparently he's willing to do violence to get it."

"If that's the case, why didn't you offer to let him have it?" It was clear from his tone that he didn't buy what she was saying. They reached his door, and he opened it to allow her inside.

Tess shook her head. "Giving him the statue wouldn't work. It would only make things worse."

"How do you know? Who is he? Why would he want the statue if it's cursed? If you're going to tell me a wild story like this and expect me to believe it, you'd better be more consistent."

"He's a Gypsy," Tess said. "That's the only explanation that makes sense."

"Uh-huh." Nate dropped onto the couch and rubbed the bridge of his nose with his thumb and forefinger. He was wildly attracted to this woman, and he didn't want her to be crazy, but he was beginning to think she was. And he didn't need to be involved with a nutcase. He'd dated a paranoid schizophrenic once. She'd seemed so normal at first. Then she'd exhibited behavior he termed "fanciful." *Then* things had started to get weird. When she'd started talking to Joan of Arc, he'd been outta there.

"A Gypsy crafted the original curse," Tess said in a perfectly sane, rational tone of voice. "I seem to remember something about Gypsies being immune to it. They can use the statue's power for evil purposes."

"Are you making this up as you go along?" Nate couldn't help asking. But he was tired, and he wasn't practicing his usual restraint when dealing with a skittish subject.

Tess folded her arms and dropped into the club chair. "Just forget it."

"I'd like to, for now, anyway. I'm beat." He offered her an apologetic smile. "Listen, why don't you crash here tonight? I've got a foldout couch in my office."

"I should go home," she said, her voice cool around the edges. "I'll call a cab and have it pick me up right at your door."

Common sense dictated that Nate let her go. But something in him wouldn't release her alone into the night to take her chances. "Look, Tess, if some crazed, knife-wielding Gypsy is after that statue, I don't think you should go home alone," he said sensibly. "He might still be lurking outside, ready to follow you." He didn't believe this whacked-out story for a minute, but why take chances? After all, Tess might not be a witch, but she was incredibly—what?—*knowing*. How had she known he wanted to write a story about Moonbeam? One minute she'd been talking about her mother, the next she'd been hurling accusations at him.

"Hmm, you might have a point." She shivered. Then she yawned. "Would you mind if I used your phone to call the hospital? I want to check on Judy. Then I think I'll take you up on your offer. You can point me toward that foldout sofa you mentioned."

He nodded, relieved. This was a first for him—a beautiful woman spending the night in his apartment, in her own bed. He pointed out the phone in the kitchen, then checked all the door and window locks, just to be on the safe side.

Judy's condition was unchanged, Tess reported after calling the hospital. That, at least, was partially good news, Nate thought. Maybe by removing the cat from—he stopped himself, appalled at the direction his thoughts had taken. Was he starting to believe in this malarkey?

Like the gentleman he wasn't, Nate found clean sheets, then led Tess into his disorderly office and helped her make up the bed. At one point they both grabbed for a pillow at the same time, and their hands brushed. At that precise moment Nate had a flash of intuition himself, a distinctly X-rated one. He saw a vivid mental image of him and Tess together, naked, lying on this very bed. He smelled her perfume. He *felt* her warm breath against his neck.

They both recoiled from the accidental touch at the same time and stared at each other.

Must be the cognac, Nate thought, though liquor had never given him hallucinations before.

Then Tess laughed self-consciously, breaking the spell. "Sorry. I'm behaving as if you're Jack the Ripper or something."

"Forget it," he said, glad that for once her sharp, observant eyes had missed the hasty withdrawal of his own hand.

He yawned expansively. "See you in the morning, okay? If you're up before me, feel free to make coffee. I can't hold my eyes open another second."

"Me, neither." She gave him an oblique, thoughtful look as he retreated from his office. "Thanks for your help tonight. I might've, um, overreacted a few minutes ago. You're not Jack the Ripper, just a sneaky reporter, and there are worse things."

"Thanks. I think." Talk about damning with faint praise.

He headed for his bedroom, stripped hastily, and flopped into his unmade bed, figuring that after the day he'd had, he would sleep for a week. Then he proceeded to stare at a wrinkle in his pillowcase for what seemed like hours, his mind awhirl, his body primed for something that wasn't *about* to happen.

Tess awoke feeling much more clearheaded. She took a shower, and even though she had to put on yesterday's clothes afterward, she still felt fresh and quick-witted.

Nate's bedroom door was closed, so she figured he must still be asleep. Rather than wake him, she wandered around his living room to see what she could learn about him. She resisted the urge to use her gift to glean information. That somehow didn't seem fair when he couldn't do the same with her. Instead, she relied on the old-fashioned tools of observation and logic.

He liked to read—everything from Mark Twain to Stephen King, and *lots* of biographies and other nonfiction. He also had an extensive and varied CD collection, including Bach, Al Jarreau, and . . . Twisted Sister? And magazines. He subscribed to everything Publisher's Clearinghouse offered.

His furniture was good-quality stuff, though not the latest style. He went for neutral colors, clean lines. His housekeeping was adequate, though not compulsive. Dust lurked in some of the more remote corners of the room.

On to the kitchen, a little square of linoleum barely big enough to turn around in. Standard bachelor fare here, including the obligatory six-pack of beer, some stale bagels, one lonely egg, ketchup. Toaster pastries. Chocolate-nut bars. A half-empty gallon of ice cream. So he had a sweet tooth.

Beyond that, she couldn't draw any conclusions except that he was a typical guy when it came to feeding himself.

A gurgling noise behind her made her jump and gasp. She whirled around, expecting to see something awful. Instead she found the coffeemaker. She could only conclude that her host was indeed awake. Her suspicions were confirmed when she heard the front door open and close. She peeked around the corner of the kitchen to see Nate standing in the living room, wearing nothing but a pair of gray sweatpants and running shoes, studying the front page of the paper. A damp T-shirt was slung around his neck.

The skin of his torso looked so smooth and tan, she found herself wanting, actually *wanting*, to lay her palms against it and feel the warmth and vitality beneath them.

Though she was positive she hadn't made a sound, he looked up. "You're awake."

She nodded. "You've been outside?"

"Went for my run."

"How was it?"

"Fine. Oh, you mean, did anything bad happen? No. I wasn't struck by lightning, no garbage trucks tried to run me over, and I especially didn't see any knife-wielding Gypsies bent on mayhem."

Tess realized she was holding her breath. She released it, focusing on slow, steady breathing for a few seconds. He was making fun of her, but her relief that nothing had happened to him overrode her irritation. Anyway, she'd learned as a child, ostracized from her peers because of her strange ways, not to respond to teasing. "I'm glad you're all right," she said sincerely.

He laid the paper down on the coffee table and came toward where she lurked in the kitchen doorway. "Were you really worried about me?" he asked. He stood close enough to her that she could smell the faint muskiness of a healthy male after exertion. The scent was surprisingly pleasant. She could almost feel her hormones bursting into bloom, her own body producing answering pheromones.

"Um, yes," she managed. "I know you don't take this curse stuff seriously, but I do."

"I'll admit, you had me a little spooked last night. But it's a lot less scary, now that the sun is shining. It's a beautiful day out there."

He flashed her a grin, then slipped past her into the kitchen. He grabbed a mug from a stand, then pulled the half-filled carafe away from the coffeemaker and stuck the cup directly under the spigot without spilling a drop.

"You like coffee?" he asked. "I made enough for two."

"Yeah. Thanks. Unlike certain impatient people, though, I don't mind waiting till it's brewed." She found herself smiling at the sheer irrepressibility of her host.

He smiled back, then sobered. "Have you checked on Judy this morning?"

She was ashamed to say she hadn't.

He put the coffee carafe back where it belonged, then handed her the cup he'd just filled. "Here. I'll make the call this time."

"I wrote the number down on the pad by your phone."

She sipped the dark, exotic brew. Kenyan. She always thought of elephants when she drank Kenyan coffee. That's how she knew. She found a chair at the small dining table tucked into a corner of the living room.

"Her condition is still listed as serious," Nate reported after he'd hung up. "But she's hanging in there."

Tess swallowed the tightness in her throat. They simply had to beat this curse thing, once and for all, or they would lose Judy. Then, who could tell who the next victim might be? Nate, herself, or whatever heir Judy had named in her will? But to defeat the curse, she needed some specialized help. Tess by herself wasn't strong enough or knowledgeable enough to take the right course.

She knew only one person who was.

Nate left her alone for a few minutes while he took his shower. When he came back into the living room, smelling of soap and shaving cream, Tess took a long, slow breath of him. For some reason, the pure, male essence of him was comforting.

"So," he said, "last night you said you'd help me

get this statue out of my trunk and out of our lives. I was thinking—if we ground it up—"

"Good heavens, no!" Tess objected. "Then each piece of the statue would carry the curse. We would magnify the evil hundreds of times."

Nate shrugged. "Guess I don't know curse protocol. Okay, then, what if we drive out to some deserted woods and bury it six feet deep?"

"I don't think that would do it. Regardless of where it is, it would still belong to us. And we might unwittingly do harm to the person who owns the land."

Nate scratched his head. "We're kind of running out of options here, kid. What do *you* suggest? Remember, you did offer to help me get rid of the cat."

Tess couldn't believe what she was about to suggest. But Nate was right—they *were* running out of options. "I think we're heading at this thing from the wrong angle. The trick isn't to get rid of the cat. We have to get rid of the curse."

He looked at her skeptically. She'd known all along that he didn't believe in the curse, that he was humoring her, but still, his obvious skepticism stung. She didn't want him to think she was certifiable.

"And how, pray tell, does one get rid of a curse?" Nate asked.

"I haven't the vaguest idea. But I know someone who would know."

"Yeah? Who's that? 'Cause I'm not too keen on involving anyone else."

"You just don't want anyone else to think you believe in curses and magic," she challenged him.

He shrugged. "Well, there's that."

"Don't worry. The person I want to visit couldn't possibly think you're crazy, 'cause she's crazy enough for all three of us." Tess tried to smile. She didn't want to scare Nate away from her plan. Sometimes even the bravest of men were reduced to quivering when faced with insanity.

"You mean Morganna?"

Nate, clever guy that he was, had figured it out. And he didn't appear even slightly hesitant. In fact, his eyes gleamed with anticipation.

SIX

Nate could hardly believe his luck. He'd searched everywhere for the whereabouts of Morganna Majick, with no luck. An interview with her would add an important dimension to his story about Moonbeam.

If he actually went through with the story.

He still wanted to, but he'd realized the night before that he would have to use care if he wanted to keep from hurting Tess. She'd raised a valid point about protecting her reputation for the sake of her career.

Well, he could continue doing research, couldn't he? He'd sort out the details and the ethics later. "So, Morganna's still around."

"She's around," Tess said with a grimace. "At the Dowling Mental Health Facility. Her official diagnosis is schizophrenia. But if you ask me, she's just plain old possessed."

"Plain old, huh?" As if possession were an everyday occurrence. "Spirits? Demons? That kind of thing?"

"No! I'm not talking *The Exorcist* here. It's just that, well, there's someone else inside her, someone mean and evil. Not the mother I remember from my early childhood. Mildred DeWitt was kind and loving and, well, open-minded. Okay, she was a little weird. But then she started calling herself Morganna, and she changed completely."

"When she found the Crimson Cat?"

"Yes, exactly then."

Nate pondered this new information. It was possible, he supposed, that if Tess's mother had believed in the curse herself, then after she'd found the cat, she'd psyched herself into her current state. Kind of like the way voodoo worked—the victim of a curse has to know about it. Then his or her own subconscious creates a self-fulfilling prophecy.

All right, so he didn't know much about it, but it was an angle to be investigated. "You think she might know how to deactivate the curse?" He realized he had a vested interest in this thing now. If the stupid statue had driven Morganna crazy, who was to say the same thing couldn't happen to Tess? He couldn't bear that thought.

"I think she *does* know, at least in theory," Tess said thoughtfully. "She tried once. I remember. But it didn't work."

"Then what makes you think—"

"Because there was something missing from whatever spell she cast. She didn't have all the pieces put together right or something. Maybe, if she could tell us how it's supposed to be done, *we* could do it."

Nate tried to stretch his mind around these concepts, but he couldn't do it. What Tess suggested was just too far-out. She wanted them to cast a *spell*, for crying out loud? He realized he was shaking his head before he'd made any conscious decision to do so.

"Okay, I know you're skeptical, and I don't blame you," Tess said. "But I really need your help with this. I'd do it by myself, but the more people you have working on a piece of magic with the same mind, the better your results. At least, that's what I was always told. I don't have a lot of practical experience with conjuring, myself."

Magic? Conjuring? Nate's head was spinning. What if his friends found out he was dabbling in witchcraft? Or worse, one of his editors? He'd be the laughing-stock of the entire journalistic community. He would have to move out of Boston and change his name.

"I want to help, really," he said. "But this is pretty far into the Twilight Zone."

She looked at him with her soulful blue eyes, and Nate felt that old kick in the gut. And suddenly he wanted to do anything for her. No wonder pretty females found it so easy to wrap him around their little fingers.

"Do you believe in psychic energy?" she asked suddenly. " 'Cause that's all I'm talking about. Witchcraft, magic, conjuring, it's all about energy."

"Well . . . I guess I don't disbelieve in it," Nate hedged. He'd had a hunch or two in his lifetime that had paid off. Sometimes he knew who was on the other end of the phone before he picked it up. Sometimes he knew what would be in the mail before the postman arrived. But that was more along the line of gut instinct. Still, wasn't she talking about a matter of degree?

"If I prove to you that psychic energy exists, will you go with me to see my mother? Help me do the magic, if I can figure out how?"

Now he had her. Proof was a pretty high order. To him, proof meant the scientific method. Repeatable results. "Okay, sure. You show me some magic—real magic, not a parlor trick—and I'll help you any way I can. But if I do, will you let me write my story?"

"I can't really stop you, can I?" she said, paling beneath her already fair complexion.

"But I don't want to do it without your cooperation." Oh, man, was he getting soft in his old age or what? "I can shield your identity."

She was silent for a long time, studying her neat, blunt fingernails. "I'll think about it," she finally said. "First, the magic. And I'll tell you, I don't like doing this because it makes me feel like a trick poodle. But it's necessary in this instance."

She looked around the room thoughtfully. "I need you to find an object that I couldn't possibly know anything about, and hand it to me."

"Any object?"

"Something that has significance to you."

"Okay." This could be fun. He scanned his bookshelves, finally spying the perfect item for this experiment—an ugly little ceramic frog. She couldn't possibly guess the complicated history behind the deceptively simple-looking figurine.

Tess took the frog, held it between her hands, inhaled deeply, and closed her eyes. When she opened them again after several long seconds, they had that otherworldly look he was becoming familiar with.

"I see something that doesn't make a lot of sense to me," she said, "but maybe it will to you. I see lemons. And I see a little towheaded boy in a red-and-white T-shirt. I sense some anger over the object, then laughter. Then a sort of . . . void."

Nate was sure his heart had stopped beating.

"Does that mean anything to you?"

He had to struggle to get the words out. "My little sister, Cathy, made the frog in her art class." He remembered that day so clearly, as if it had just happened the previous week. His tomboy sister, wearing her favorite red-and-white shirt, her hair cut boyishly short. She'd brought the frog home, so proud, and Nate had told her it was the ugliest frog he'd ever seen. She'd poured a pitcher of lemonade over his head and had stopped speaking to him for days. As adults, they'd laughed over the incident.

After her death several years earlier, he'd wanted nothing from her effects except the stupid frog.

He took the frog away from Tess, illogically affronted that she should pry into his memories. "Could have been a lucky guess," he said.

"Give me something else, then. I can do this all day."

He gave her a framed photograph of his grandfather, looking dapper in a bow tie and bowler hat.

"Steel mills," she said. "And I smell pipe tobacco—Turkish pipe tobacco. Broken collarbone. Does the name Alexander mean anything?"

"How are you doing that?" Nate demanded, snatching the photo away. Everything she'd said was dead on the money. His grandfather, Alexander Wagner, had grown up in Allentown and had worked in the steel mills. He'd smoked a Turkish pipe. He'd broken his collarbone during a fall, shortly before his death. Tess was scaring the hell out of him.

"The same way I found out you were writing a story about me. I inadvertently picked up your notebook. The answers come through my hands in the form of vibrations that I—"

"No. No way. I'm not buying this."

"You are one tough customer." She sighed, sounding bored. "Give me something else."

Almost desperately, he handed her a book of matches.

"Dinner." She licked her lips, then wrinkled her nose. "Caesar salad. Steak, rare. Very pretty blonde in a white silk dress. She wears Opium perfume, I think. Mm, I'm sorry."

"About what?" he asked warily.

"She dumped you that night."

"She did not dump me. *I'm* the one who broke it off. She was getting too demanding, always making me take her to those expensive places, ordering bottles of wine and then not drinking them. I—". Nate cut himself off as he realized what he was saying. He looked at Tess, really looked at her. "You really *are* a witch!"

She gave him a somewhat pitying look back. "You'll get used to it."

Since Tess refused to let Nate move the cat statue from its resting place in his trunk, and since she also refused to go anywhere in the car while the cat was there, she allowed him to talk her into taking his motorcycle to the sanitarium where her mother lived.

The day had cleared and warmed up, so the elements weren't a problem. The problem was putting her arms around Nate's waist. Well, there was no help for it, she thought as she gingerly grabbed onto his belt loops. Anyway, she'd touched him before and nothing terrible had happened. His vibrations were starting to feel familiar to her. Even pleasant.

As they made the thirty-minute trip out to Braintree, where the sanitarium was located, she focused on the passing scenery. But Nate's essence was always there, simmering in the back of her mind, taunting her with sensual images that would take over her whole consciousness in a heartbeat if she let them.

But she never let them, not entirely. If she had, the experience would have swamped her, overwhelmed her, knocked her clean off the bike. To her delight, she discovered that she could control the sensations if she applied herself. She remembered a long-ago lecture her mother had given her about learning to control her powers and shield herself from negative energies, but at the time she'd been disinterested, preferring to avoid those negative vibes rather than managing them.

At the time she'd hated the gift that made her so different from other children and had no intention of developing it, the way her mother wanted her to.

She wished now that she'd listened. Then she would have a better idea of what was going on. All she knew was that for the first time in her life she was holding on to another human being for an extended length of time, and the experience was not unpleasant. A surge of hope filled her, despite her current dire circumstances, despite the terrible task that lay ahead of her.

Tess directed Nate to turn down the long, tree-lined avenue toward the private sanitarium where Mildred DeWitt had resided for the past fifteen years. It was expensive, but despite the DeWitt family's problems, they'd had money. Tess's father, who'd died when she was two, had left a sizable estate and life-insurance benefits. Tess and her mother had lived simply, so there had been plenty left when "Morganna" had been committed. Although she'd only been thirteen, Tess and her guardian, a cool and disinterested paternal aunt, had put the money into a trust for her mother's care.

The sight of the lovely old redbrick building, with its stately white columns and huge oak trees, filled her with a sense of dread. She'd approached the sanitarium countless times over the years, always hoping that things would be different. Each time her hopes were dashed.

Nate pulled the motorcycle into a space in the visitor parking area and cut the engine. Somewhere a bird called. An oriole, Tess thought. When she'd been a child, she and her mother had spent hours walking the countryside, gathering the herbs and wildflowers needed for various concoctions. Mildred had patiently schooled her distracted daughter on how to recognize local species of flora and fauna.

Some of it had stuck, Tess realized. She could still recognize certain birdcalls and wildflowers.

"These are some digs," Nate commented as he helped Tess off the huge bike. He stowed their helmets in a compartment on the back of the Harley. "Is it as comfortable inside as it looks from out here?"

"All the comforts of home," she quipped. He would see soon enough. For all its luxurious trappings, Tess had always considered Dowling a chamber of horrors. Though she assiduously avoided touching anything while she was there, the vibrations assaulted her anyway—so many lost souls, confused, sad. No matter how qualified the nurses and doctors, no matter how kind and caring the attendants, the very air smelled of desolation.

The star horror was Morganna herself.

The front entrance hall could have belonged to a luxury hotel, with its shiny black-and-white tile floor and a chandelier that probably weighed more than Nate's Harley. Except for the wheelchairs that lined one wall.

An elegant woman in a power suit appeared from nowhere to greet them. "Good morning. May I help you?"

"I'm Tess DeWitt. I'm here to see my mother, Mildred DeWitt."

"Oh, Tess, of course. I didn't recognize you at first. You haven't been here in a while."

Tess didn't bother to explain her prolonged absence. What good did driving all the way there do, when Morganna refused visitors? Tess had stopped counting back to figure out how long it had been since she'd last laid eyes on her mother, but she suspected it had been more than three years this time. In all the years she'd been here, Morganna had tolerated her daughter's presence maybe half a dozen times, and then only for five or ten minutes.

"I'll check with your mother's nurse and see if she's receiving visitors today," the woman said, as if Morganna were a duchess instead of a patient in a mental institution. "You may have a seat in the parlor." She gestured with one long, well-manicured hand, then turned smartly on her heel.

"Receiving visitors?" Nate repeated when the woman was out of earshot.

"I probably should have warned you. Morganna doesn't like me much. She would prefer for me to leave her alone, but I keep coming back, like a dog that doesn't mind getting kicked if there's even a chance he might get a pat."

Instead of offering words of sympathy or pity, which she would have hated, Nate simply asked, "Why doesn't she like you?"

"She blames me. I took it as long as I could. But when Child Protective Services launched an investiga-

tion of our home life, I told them everything. I guess I didn't realize the repercussions. Suddenly we were swimming in social workers, investigators, lawyers, doctors. They took me away from her."

"That wasn't what you wanted?"

She shook her head. "I wanted someone to bring my real mother back, that's all. In retrospect, I suppose the authorities did the best they could. And I was somewhat relieved to be out of that house." She shivered even thinking about the gloomy nightmare her once-happy home had become. "But I hadn't realized that I would be cut off from her completely, by her own choice."

"What if she won't see you today?"

As in answer to his question, a nurse dressed in old-fashioned whites and a cap appeared in the parlor. "Tess."

"Heidi. It's nice to see you again." Tess stood and took the nurse's hands in hers. Heidi Pavel, Morganna's primary nurse for several years now, smiled in greeting.

But Heidi's smile didn't last long. "I'm afraid she won't see you," she said. "She's actually having a pretty good day, in terms of lucidity, but she doesn't want visitors."

Tess sighed. She simply had to get in to see Morganna. "Heidi, will you do me a favor?" she asked impulsively. "Will you go back to my mother and tell her I've found the Crimson Cat, and that I need her help?"

Heidi looked puzzled, but she nodded. "I can try."

She turned and left, her crepe-soled shoes squeaking against the polished linoleum as she walked.

"You think that'll work?" asked Nate, who'd been standing by anxiously watching Tess's exchange with the nurse.

"If she remembers the Cat, she'll be intrigued enough to find out how I became involved with it. If she doesn't remember it . . ." Tess shrugged. "Then I was wrong. She can't help us."

Heidi returned almost immediately, smiling warmly this time. "Apparently those were the magic words. Your mother said to send you back." She lowered her voice. "What's a crimson cat, anyway?"

"Trust me, you don't want to know," Nate said.

Nate followed Tess as she led him unerringly down a maze of hallways, enjoying the gentle sway of her hips beneath the cotton print skirt. Certainly he would rather look at Tess's backside than the other choices available to him—the residents of Dowling.

They sat in wheelchairs along the wide hallways, strapped in or down. They stared with glassy eyes at the wall, or carried on loud and imaginative conversations with nonexistent friends. One woman shouted obscenities as they passed.

Nate shivered. He was a journalist. He was supposed to be inured to the harsh realities of life. But this place made him feel worse than the meanest streets he'd ever walked. He knew this was probably the best care available to the mentally ill. He also knew that it would make him feel awful to have a loved one locked up there.

Tess strode onward, seemingly oblivious. She said hi to one old man who greeted her with a wave and a big, toothless smile, but other than that, she didn't interact. As sensitive as she was, he figured she had to work pretty hard to distance herself from all this. But that was apparently what she'd done, or what she was trying to do.

He was still a little blown away by this "psychic energy" business. But she'd proved, to his exacting standards, that she received information from some other source than the normal five senses. Some might call him a gullible fool for believing in any sort of hocus-pocus, but better gullible than downright stupid. To ignore the evidence she'd provided him would be stupid.

So, Tess was psychic. And the feats she'd demonstrated on television as a preadolescent hadn't been tricks. He was still numb from the realization. But he was also intrigued. If there really was such a thing as psychic energy, then the world as Nate knew it had just turned upside down. If the impossible was suddenly not only possible, but palpably real, then who was he to say that a Gypsy curse from a couple of centuries ago was hogwash?

Tess finally stopped at one of the gleaming white doors, which was open a crack. She tapped on it with her knuckles. "Morganna?"

No answer came from within. Just a blood-chilling cackle.

Tess apparently took the laughter as a signal for her to enter. "Good morning, Morganna," she said, her voice carefully modulated as she slowly entered the room. "Thank you for seeing me."

"Don't thank me till the visit's done," Morganna said ominously.

Nate was struck by his first glimpse of the woman, who bore little resemblance to the exotic creature he'd seen on the videotape of the *Don Woodland Show*. Morganna Majick was a haggard shell of a woman, bent, emaciated. Her hair, a mixture of light brown and snow white, hung in limp shanks halfway down her back. Nate remembered her hair as being jet-black, the way her daughter's had been on the TV show. They both must've dyed their hair for effect.

Morganna's clothing, a black, shapeless caftan, befitted a witch. She couldn't have been much over fifty, but she looked closer to seventy.

Her sharp, birdlike eyes caught sight of Nate, and she smiled, revealing small, white teeth that appeared sharpened, like an animal's. "Whom have we here?" she exclaimed in mock delight. "A boyfriend? I don't think Moonbeam's ever had a boyfriend before, have you, darling?"

Tess's face was hard, impassive, and she stayed well out of touching distance of her mother. "I doubt you would know, since you haven't seen me in three years. But he's not a boyfriend," she said firmly.

Her words had a deflating effect on Nate. Of course he wasn't a boyfriend, but she didn't have to say it as if it were an irrevocable condition.

Tess took a deep breath, starting fresh. "Morganna, this is Nate Wagner. By a strange set of circumstances, the Crimson Cat is now in the trunk of his car."

Morganna ignored Nate's outstretched hand. "Ooh, the Crimson Cat. Yes, now we're getting down to it, aren't we? The nasty beast." She continued to stare at Nate. "Does she touch you, boyfriend? Couldn't get her to touch me nor anyone, the fey little thing. Soon as she finished suckling, she'd have nothing to do with me."

"Mother, please," Tess said impatiently, her face flushed with embarrassment. "This visit isn't about me, and Nate isn't my boyfriend, all right?"

" 'Mother' now, is it?" Morganna turned her sharp gaze toward her daughter. "Trying to soften up your old lady? After all the years of neglect, now suddenly you need the old witch. So it's 'Mother.' "

"It slipped out," Tess said stoically. "You're the one who doesn't want me to call you that. I've always tried to honor your wishes, but sometimes I forget."

A surge of protectiveness rose up inside Nate, along with an overblown irritation toward Morganna, a mentally ill woman, for all the pain she'd caused her daughter over the years. How had Tess referred to it? Radically dysfunctional?

Abruptly the light of mean-spirited amusement went out of Morganna's eyes. She drifted over to her bed and sat down on the edge, as if she were alone in the room. She stared up at the ceiling. "What do you want, girl?"

"It's the Crimson Cat," Tess said quickly, taking

advantage of Morganna's momentary lucidity. "We found it accidentally in an antique store, and my friend Judy bought it even though I told her not to, and now she's sick, maybe dying. Nate and I removed the statue from her apartment, but it hasn't helped."

"Of course not," Morganna said curtly. "Once the curse takes firm hold, there's no stopping it."

"But there is," Tess insisted, sitting beside her mother. "You tried once. I remember."

Morganna shook her head vehemently. "Tried and failed."

"Because something was missing, you said."

"It was a long time ago," Morganna said wearily. "I don't remember."

"You could try," Nate wheedled.

Morganna jerked her gaze up to stare at him, panic-stricken. "Don't you see? If you try to defeat the curse, the Cat will take vengeance. Do you want to end up like me? Let it rest. Hide the statue in a closet and forget about it. A life of bad luck is better than no life at all."

"I can't let it rest," Tess said, her eyes filling. "I brought this thing on. Now Judy's dying, and I've involved Nate too. I have to try to undo it."

"You've had no training," Morganna argued. She again turned to Nate. "She denied my training. She was born with the natural talent of a true master, much better than me, but she'd have nothing to do with it. It was her *birthright*."

They were all quiet for a long time until Tess said softly, "I wanted to be normal."

"You can't be." Morganna smiled, showing her strange teeth, and it chilled Nate to his marrow. "The Dark Lord will find you. He's already found you. It's only a matter of time before you're his." She held out one bony hand to Tess. "It will be so much easier if you come willingly."

"No!" Tess jumped to her feet and moved to the far corner of the room, as far as she could get from Morganna. "Maybe the curse will defeat me. But I won't go without a fight. Tell me how to fight it, Morganna. You have the tools. I have abilities; you just said so. At least give me a chance!"

Nate watched the currents arcing between mother and daughter. He could swear that the air had become charged. The hairs on his arms were standing on end. And he felt the first stirrings of fear, real fear. If this was a delusion, it was a damn powerful one.

Morganna sighed wearily. "You can try, I suppose, for what good it will do. But I warn you, if the spell doesn't kill you, the curse will."

"It's a chance I'm willing to take," Tess said.

"I don't have it with me, of course." She turned to Nate. "They didn't let me take anything with me when they brought me here."

"But there is a spell?" Tess asked anxiously. "Written down somewhere?"

"In my Book of Shadows."

Tess inhaled sharply. "Oh, no."

SEVEN

"Oh, no, what?" Nate asked. "What's a Book of Shadows?"

Tess trembled visibly. Nate was afraid she might keel over, but instead she sank onto the nearest surface, a footstool. "It's a grimoire. A witch's spell book."

Nate sure hoped his pocket tape recorder was picking all this up. He hadn't wanted to carry a notepad for fear of stymieing discussion between the two women. Of course, there was no way he would forget any of this. It was all too weird.

"Where is this book?" Nate asked. He had a feeling he wasn't going to like the answer.

"At home," Morganna said. "The home they took away from me when they took my daughter and everything else." She narrowed her eyes at Tess. "Your fault. Evil child!"

Tess reacted as if she'd been slapped.

Nate's impulse was to protect her from the foul-tempered old biddy, to defend her against the verbal assault. But he bit his tongue. The seeds of this mother-daughter relationship had been sown years ago. It wasn't up to him to fix it, as if he could.

"You ruined my life, you little wretch!" Morganna screeched. "Get out! It would serve you right if that cursed Cat destroyed you and all you love!"

Nate didn't wait around to hear anymore. "We're going now," he said in a tone of voice that invited no arguments. He grabbed Tess's arm, opened the door to the hallway, and virtually dragged her outside. Morganna's voice, moaning something about a full moon, followed them.

As soon as Morganna was safely closed away behind her door, Tess leaned her back against the wall and dropped her head into her hands.

"That was pretty rough," Nate said, because he couldn't think of anything more brilliant.

Tess sniffed in response. Aw, hell, she was crying. Nate never knew what to do in these circumstances. Maybe distracting her would work. He started to ask her more about this Book of Shadows business, but just then the nurse they'd talked to earlier came sailing down the hall, scowling.

"What happened?" she demanded. "I heard Mrs. DeWitt." She cast an anxious glance at the closed door.

Tess composed herself. "I'm afraid I've upset her—again."

"It's not your fault," Heidi said, though Nate wasn't sure she believed it. "Mrs. DeWitt upsets easily. Still, maybe this visit wasn't such a good idea. I hadn't thought about it, but maybe talking about your lost pet made her . . . anxious."

"Her pet?" Nate and Tess asked together.

"The crimson cat?"

Tess actually laughed. "Trust me, the Crimson Cat isn't a pet." She sobered. "We have to go now, Heidi. Please call me if there's anything I can do where my mother's concerned. Otherwise . . . well, I don't know if I'll be coming back again."

Heidi gave her a compassionate look. "No one would blame you, sweetie, if you didn't."

As soon as they were back out into the bright sun and fresh air, Tess took a deep, cleansing breath. "I'm sorry you had to be there for that, Nate."

"I'm sorry if I made matters worse." He started to put a comforting hand on her shoulder. Out of habit, she skittered away before he could touch her.

"Why do you keep doing that?" he asked. "I don't bite. Am I that repulsive?" The teasing glint in his eyes told her he knew damn well he was anything but repulsive.

"It's not that," she said with a shake of her head. She decided to tell him what her problem was. "You know how I pick up vibrations from objects by holding them in my hands?"

"Uh-huh."

"Well, it's not a voluntary thing. I pick up vibrations from whatever I touch, or whatever touches me."

"What, so you can read me like you did the frog

and the picture and the matches?" He crossed his arms in a classic pose of incredulity.

" 'Fraid so. I don't do it on purpose. It just happens."

"Does that mean you can read my mind?" He looked decidedly worried.

"It's not an exact thing. I pick up impressions, or a word here and there. Actually, I've found it's not so bad, touching you."

"Gee, thanks."

"No, I mean, your vibrations are kind of in sync with mine, if that makes any sense. But they can be a little overwhelming, and I'm still trying to shake off everything that came at me inside." She nodded her head toward the redbrick building behind them.

"So you pick up vibes from everything? Clothes, food, furniture—"

"Exactly. My mother used to tell me that I needed to learn how to control my abilities, to shut them off, but I didn't listen. I thought if I just ignored them, they would go away and I could be normal." She heard the wistfulness in her own voice.

Nate shook his head. "That must be a helluva way to live," he said dubiously.

"If I'm careful, it's not so bad. C'mon, let's go. This place gives me the creeps."

"Yeah, me, too, and I"m not the least bit psychic."

"You might be surprised," she said, smiling at his startled expression. She took off for the parking lot. "Are you up for a visit to Judy? Or do you need to do some work?"

"For now, you *are* my work."

"Oh." She wasn't sure why that revelation disappointed her so. He'd made it clear he still wanted to write his story, regardless of her objections. "Then let's stop by my place so I can change clothes. We can pick up my car too."

"You don't like the motorcycle?"

"It's not my favorite mode of transportation."

Three hours later Nate was still hanging in there with her. He'd taken her to her condo so she could change into jeans and a comfortable cable-knit sweater. While waiting, he'd stood in her living room, hardly moving, as if he was afraid he might disturb or sully something in her white-on-white decor.

Just in case, she chucked a change of clothes into an overnight bag. She didn't know when she might return home, and she wanted to be prepared.

Next they'd taken Tess's car to the hospital. Judy had been sleeping fitfully. Her parents were there, looking much older and more frail than Tess remembered them. But at least she could leave the hospital knowing someone who loved Judy would be there when she woke up. If she woke up. Her vitals were slipping. The doctors were talking about putting her on a respirator.

"What's next?" Nate asked as they climbed into Tess's Toyota Tercel in the hospital visitors' lot.

"We have to find the Book of Shadows."

"Is there any chance of that? After fifteen years? Surely whoever bought your mother's house got rid of the book."

"No one bought the house. It was on the market for a while, but it didn't sell."

"You mean you still own it?"

"Yes. It's over in Sudbury. I suspect it's still standing, if it didn't burn down. I have the keys." She jangled her keyring before inserting the car key into the ignition and starting the engine. "Are you game?"

"Sure."

Now, as they turned off U.S. 90 and headed toward the town where Tess had grown up, her unease began to build. Nothing bad had happened to them all day— at least, nothing curse-wise. No car accidents or flat tires or injuries. Yet Tess couldn't shake this feeling of impending tragedy. It was almost as if the Cat were resting up for bigger and better things.

Or maybe it was just Tess's dread over facing her childhood home. She and Morganna had been relatively happy there once. But darker memories overshadowed the nicer ones. She hadn't been back to the house since Child Protective Services had taken her away.

Nate had been quiet for most of the drive, perhaps picking up on her mood and matching it. She hadn't been kidding about him being psychic. Of course, she believed that everyone had some extrasensory abilities. But Nate had a strong sensitivity to people that he probably wasn't even aware of. It was what made him a good reporter, she imagined. His hunches would tell him whom to pursue and what questions to ask. His ability to match the mood or mind-set of anybody he talked to would make him likable and cause others to open up to him, as she had done.

As Tess turned down her old street, with the incongruously innocent name of Apple Blossom Road, her anxiety increased. What had she gotten herself into? She'd been close to a nervous breakdown when she'd finally left this place. Was she going to regress right back to that state the moment she saw the house? Or just flip out completely and scare Nate to pieces?

Around the final turn, she held her breath. She would have closed her eyes, too, if she hadn't been driving. God, there it was, in all its menacing glory. A faded "For Sale" sign, the phone number almost illegible, leaned in the front yard. She turned into the crushed-shell driveway and stopped the car.

"This is it, huh?"

Tess nodded. She forced herself to look at the house, to study it. Most of the windows were boarded up, and the shrubs and vines had grown out of control, but otherwise the structure appeared sound. It was just a house, two stories, white frame, a big front porch with pillars that had once looked inviting. Now it reminded Tess of a gaping mouth with teeth missing.

"You ready?" he asked. "If you don't want to go inside, I'll do it. Just tell me what to look for and where."

"No, I'll come," she said, opening her door. She had to put one foot consciously in front of the other to advance her toward the house. She almost felt like she was wading through molasses.

Nate bounded up the front steps ahead of her, disturbing a flock of pigeons having a siesta on the porch. "This is a great old house. I can't believe it didn't sell."

"I can." She didn't need to elaborate. As soon as she twisted the key in the rusty old lock and pushed the door open, a sickly odor greeted them—the smell of dust and cobwebs, small dead things, disuse, and evil. Of course, Tess didn't imagine that Nate interpreted the smell as she did. But judging from the way he recoiled, he found it repugnant.

He coughed. "God! How long has this place been closed up?"

"Years, I'm afraid." She stepped gingerly over the threshold. The entrance-hall floor was littered with plaster that had fallen from the ceiling.

Nate flipped on a light switch. Nothing happened. "Too much to hope for, I guess. Are the walls . . . black?"

"Uh-huh. One of Morganna's little idiosyncrasies."

"Hmm."

They moved into the living room. Most of her mother's things were still there, covered in yellowed sheets that resembled ghosts in the half-light. Those things not draped were caked with dust. Nate gallantly broke through all the cobwebs ahead of Tess.

"Do you have any idea where to look?" he asked as they moved slowly through the room, their feet crunching against the debris-strewn wood floors.

"Not really. Morganna kept her grimoire hidden. It's a very private thing, a Book of Shadows. She wouldn't have wanted just anyone stumbling across it."

"Including you?"

"Especially me. She said that without training, I could really make a mess of her spells."

"Okay. Where do people hide things? How about under her bed?"

Tess shrugged. "It's worth a try."

"Why don't we split up? I'll go upstairs—"

"No!" Panic rose hot in her throat. She decided not to put on a brave front. "Don't you dare leave me here alone."

"You're scared?"

"Hell, yes. Aren't you?"

"I'm a guy. Guys aren't supposed to get scared." He paused, looking around. "I'm uneasy, though. I'll admit that. All this place needs is a few bats, and the Munsters would feel right at home. Is that a black candle?"

"Uh-huh. There's a pentagram under the rug too. There used to be some really weird stuff, but I guess the real-estate people packed it away before putting the house up for sale. I remember they wanted us to have it repainted so it would bring a better price, but my guardian didn't want to mess with it."

"Who was your guardian?"

"An aunt. My father's sister. She didn't want me. I hardly saw her after I went away to college, and she died a few years ago. Still, living with her was better than living here."

"Poor Tess," Nate murmured.

She didn't want him to feel sorry for her, she realized. Pity wasn't something she was prepared to accept from Nate Wagner. She also realized she wanted something else from him, something beyond his help with this magic business. She wasn't sure what that something was, but it filled her with a yearning that was completely alien to her.

She felt a cold draft and shivered. "Let's get to work. You're right, we should split up. You go upstairs. I'll start down here."

"If you're sure?"

She nodded. He lightly stroked her arm in a gesture of understanding, then jerked his hand back. "Sorry. I know you don't like to be touched, but it's sort of instinctual with me to reach out to you when you're hurting."

"You don't have to be sorry. Please don't. . . ." She was so confused, her throat hurt. She remembered what her mother had said, about how Tess never allowed anyone to touch her. She'd never before considered how her aversion to touch must have affected Morganna. It must have made her feel rejected, unloved, particularly because Tess never really explained it to her mother.

"You can touch me if you want," she said now to Nate. Impulsively she grabbed his hand and brought it up to her face. *What am I doing?* She looked up into his eyes, and for a moment all else receded—the house and all it represented, the curse, everything. There were only the two of them in this great vacuum, with waves of warmth pulsating back and forth between them.

It was so amazing, how he made her feel, as if she were in a protective cocoon, or bathing in warm lotion. But it went beyond that. She felt a tingling deep in her core, a hotness between her legs that wasn't uncomfortable, exactly, but it made her want to squirm. Her palms went damp.

She was aroused. In this awful place, she was suddenly aware of herself as a woman as she had never been before.

She'd been aroused a few times in the past, so she recognized it. But the other times she'd been looking, not touching.

"I . . . I . . ." She couldn't articulate anything. He came closer, and she realized with a sense of awe mingled with fear that he was going to kiss her.

He did. Her mind exploded with pleasure, expanding to take in every outward sensation—the texture of his mouth pressing insistently against hers, the firm warmth of his hand where it had slid behind her neck, the sound of Nate's breathing, and the pounding of her own blood through her veins. The sensory overload effectively blocked out her psychic receptors. For a few moments more she reveled in the purely physical realm.

Then a fluttering sound overhead jerked her back to reality. She pulled away from Nate. "What was that?"

Nate was looking around, too. "A bat?"

"Oh, God, I hate bats. Let's find the stupid book and get out of here." She pulled away. He let her, though reluctantly, it seemed.

Since Tess knew the house better, she volunteered to face the upstairs. She rifled through her mother's old closets, looked under the bed and in bureau drawers.

Everywhere were reminders of the nightmare her life had become—pictures and statues of demons, ceremonial bones and knives, religious symbols that had been reversed or otherwise perverted. There was almost no trace left of the beautiful, gentle magic Morganna had performed when she was plain old Mildred DeWitt.

Tess became almost numb from the constant onslaught of hideous vibrations. Yet she pressed on. The book had to be somewhere.

She heard a yelp from downstairs. She ran to the landing and called down to Nate, "Hey, you okay?"

"Yeah, I'm fine," he answered sheepishly. "Are you?"

"I'm okay. Any sign of the book?"

"No."

When she finished searching the upstairs, she pulled down the attic stairs and climbed up, but all she found were a few dusty boxes with Christmas decorations that hadn't been used in twenty years. Morganna didn't believe in celebrating Christian holidays.

With no small amount of relief, Tess rejoined Nate downstairs. He was methodically checking the book titles on the shelves in the den.

"She wouldn't have kept it here in plain sight," Tess said.

Nate jumped. "Hey, don't sneak up on me like that." But he smiled at her.

"What made you yelp earlier?" she asked.

"Oh, that. I opened that closet over there, and something jumped out and tried to kill me. A devil or something. I wouldn't recommend looking."

But Tess was already drifting toward the closet. Something was teasing at her memory. She opened the door a crack. Two sightless eyes peered at her from the darkness.

"Oh, I remember!" She opened the door wider to reveal the stuffed head of a ram, complete with huge, curved horns. "It's Ernie."

"Ernie?"

"Mother bought him at a garage sale. He was our own private Horned God."

"Horned . . . you mean like the devil?" Nate asked dubiously. He came to stand behind Tess and have another look at his nemesis.

"No. He's one of the main deities of the ancient religion. The Catholic Church turned him into the devil back in the days when they were burning witches and heretics. But he's not such a bad guy, just the Goddess's consort. And . . ." Following a sudden flash of intuition, or maybe memory, Tess stepped away from the closet. "Would you mind lifting Ernie off the wall? Maybe he's guarding something."

"Sure." Nate did as she'd asked, putting the ram's head aside.

Tess stepped into the closet and started feeling around, pushing and prodding the plywood planks. Finally one of the boards gave a little under pressure, then sprang open.

"Eureka!" There was a thick, leather-bound book sitting in a niche, along with Morganna's most sacred ceremonial tools—a knife, a silver chalice, a white candle, and a censer.

"What's all that other stuff?" Nate asked, leaning into the closet to have a better look.

Tess resisted the urge to lean closer, to let just his hair brush her cheek. She was getting dangerously close to being obsessed with the idea of touching him. "Those are a witch's basic tools. The knife, or athame, represents earth; the chalice, water; the candle, fire; and the censer, air. They're used for almost all ceremonies."

"Should we take them with us?"

Tess hesitated. "No. They're Morganna's personal tools. If we need anything like that, we can buy them new."

"Okay." Nate scooped the book up. Tess noticed that, unlike everything else in the house, the Book of Shadows was scrupulously clean, without even a speck of dust to mar the tooled-leather cover. It was as if the dust were afraid to land on it.

She nixed that thought. It's just a book, she chanted silently. It can't hurt me.

"Can we go now?" Nate asked. "I don't know about you, but I could use some fresh air."

"Yeah, me too."

Nate put Ernie back into his dark home. Then, the two them moved fast to get out of the house.

Nate sat with the book on his lap while Tess drove back toward Boston, but he didn't open it or make any comment about it for several minutes. He felt embarrassingly uneasy about delving into Morganna's private world of magic and mayhem.

He was also thinking about the kiss he'd shared with Tess, and what it meant. Was she thinking about it too? Or had the practicalities of their current predicament overridden a momentary, foolish burst of passion?

Well, he'd never been one to act coy. "Are you sorry you kissed me?" he asked, just to get the ball rolling.

She turned her startled blue eyes off the road and toward him for an instant. "No. Are you? Sorry you kissed me, that is."

"No." Well, that hadn't gone much of anywhere.

"Look, Nate, I can't think about that right now. It was a nice kiss—no, a great kiss, a fantastic kiss, but I can't think about it right now. I need to be tranquil and clearheaded to work magic."

A fantastic kiss. He savored her words. What guy didn't like to be told he was a great kisser? But apparently she wasn't keen on repeating the experience anytime soon, not until she'd completed her "magic." All the more reason for him to do everything he could to assist her.

Did that make him a sorcerer's apprentice?

He opened the book. The pages were yellowed and brittle, but not crumbling. Still, he treated them gently. A number of names were inscribed in the flyleaf, the last being Morganna Majick. Oddly, the one above it was Mildred Hampton. "Was Hampton your mother's maiden name?" he asked.

"Uh-huh."

Interesting. It was almost as if Morganna thought of herself as a separate entity once she'd rechristened herself Morganna. "What am I looking for, anyway?"

"A spell for removing a curse. Or anything that sounds like it might work."

The first few pages contained sketches of various plants and flowers, and their purported medicinal qualities. "How old is this book, anyway?" Apparently it hadn't belonged to Morganna originally.

"That particular book is over a hundred years old, I imagine. But the information, particularly at the front, is much older. It was copied from my great-grandmother's grimoire, which, in turn, was copied from another ancestor's. That's why the writing is so hard to read and the wording is so peculiar."

Peculiar, to say the least. It was almost like trying to read Anglo-Saxon.

He worked his way deeper into the book. There were recipes for various brews designed to relieve stomach pain or soothe a sore tooth, to induce childbirth, to heal cuts. All pretty benevolent sounding to Nate. But gradually, as he turned the pages, the "recipes" turned more fanciful. This one kept a husband faithful, that one brought in a bountiful harvest or caused a cow to give more milk. The instructions became more complex, too, involving more than simply brewing tea. There were timetables to be met, phases of the moon to take into account.

Suddenly he remembered Morganna's parting words—something about the full moon.

"Tess, do you happen to know what phase of the moon we're in?" he asked.

"It's a waxing moon. Be full tomorrow night, I think. Why?"

"I think that might become important."

He continued reading, fascinated. He wondered if Tess would let him reproduce a few pages. They would make great graphics for his article.

His article. It was shaping up into one terrific story. Now, if he could just convince Tess that letting him write it wouldn't hurt her. He could change her name and some other pertinent details so that even her closest friends wouldn't recognize her. But he realized that now wasn't the time to talk with Tess about his story. She wouldn't want to deal with it now. She had other things on her mind—namely, taking the steps that she imagined would save her friend's life.

He glanced over at her. As they neared town the traffic had turned heavy, and she was concentrating mightily on her driving.

Nate turned another page of the grimoire and felt a sudden chill shimmy up his spine. " 'A Spell to Counteract Black Magick,' " he read aloud. "Could that be it?"

At that precise moment, as they pushed through an intersection on a yellow light, a dump truck shot toward them from the cross street. Tess slammed on the brakes and did a squealing one-eighty. Her quick reflexes prevented the truck from broadsiding them on Nate's side and possibly turning him into roadkill. But the truck still managed to clip the back bumper and send them into a light pole. Tess's hood popped open and the horn went off.

She looked over at him with wide eyes. "Yes, that's the spell."

EIGHT

No one was seriously injured, Tess reminded herself as the cops drove away and she and Nate climbed back into her car, which was drivable if a little banged up. It could have been so much worse. But she was still trembling as she put the car in gear.

"Hey, are you sure you're okay to drive?" Nate asked her, his voice full of concern. "I'll drive if you want."

"No, I'm okay." Tess heard the catch in her voice and swallowed ruthlessly to get rid of it.

"All right," Nate said. "You're thinking the curse had something to do with this. Am I correct?"

"Of course you're correct. And it did. The moment you turned to the correct page in the book, something awful happened to us."

"Awful would have been if you hadn't had a dozen witnesses who saw that the accident wasn't your fault. Awful would have been if you were driving without insurance and had to go to jail. This was bad, but it wasn't awful. It's something that happens to dozens of Bostonians every week. Get some perspective."

Tess rubbed her right temple, trying to dispel the tension residing there. "I hope you're right." Traffic was lighter, now that they'd spent the majority of rush hour filling out police reports. Because Nate's house was closer, Tess drove there.

Nate had refrained from opening the book again. She wondered if that was because of her worries, or his own reticence to tempt fate. His logical side might be keeping up a strong facade, but deep down he couldn't help but be worried about the curse. Coincidences and bad luck took one only so far.

She had a difficult time finding a parking space, but she finally managed to wedge her little car into a tiny spot in front of a Chinese take-out restaurant. The smells emanating from the restaurant were heavenly, and her stomach rumbled.

"Hungry?" Nate asked. "I'll buy dinner. We haven't eaten since breakfast, and this place has great food. Good vegetarian stuff."

She was touched that he remembered her dietary preferences. "I'm starved. And I can't concentrate on an empty stomach. By all means, let's get some dinner."

Nate ordered a vegetable deluxe dinner for her, and cashew shrimp for himself. The food appeared, packed in paper cartons with chopsticks and plenty of soy sauce, just the way she liked it. Nate paid, and she carried their dinner the four blocks to his apartment, inhaling the delectable scents. She tried not to look at Nate, carrying the Book of Shadows.

About half a block from the front entrance to his building, Nate stopped abruptly and threw one arm out in front of Tess, bumping her in the chin.

"What?"

"It's that guy again."

Instinctively, Tess ducked into a doorway. Her heart started that insistent pounding that had been so much a part of her life these past few days. "Did he see us?" She whispered, though the swarthy man was a half block away.

"I don't think so." Nate's voice sounded edgy. "What the hell does he want?"

Tess peered cautiously around the brick doorway. The man in question was loitering outside Nate's building, smoking a cigarette, acting as if he had nothing more urgent on his mind than enjoying the spring weather. But it was the same man, all right.

"I told you what he wants," Tess said impatiently. "He wants the Cat."

"Come on," Nate said, dragging her back the way they'd come. "We'll enter the building from the back. Then I'm going downstairs and have a chat with our mystery man."

They ducked into an alley, following a similar path to the one they'd taken the night before, though they went around the fence this time instead of over it.

"I don't think you should confront him," Tess said. "He's dangerous."

"Yeah, well, so am I, when someone threatens what's mine."

Tess was surprised at the deadly vehemence she detected in Nate's voice. She'd never heard him quite so . . . forceful before. She'd been thinking of him as easygoing, good-natured, quick to laugh. Now she realized she might have underestimated him. There was a hard edge to Nate Wagner, buried beneath the easy laugh and the twinkling brown eyes.

And what, precisely, did he consider "mine"? The only thing the swarthy man had threatened was Tess herself.

Something inside her trembled.

Nate put an arm around her shoulders as they made their way up the alley toward the back door of his building. Rather than shrink from his touch, she immersed herself in the sense of strength she derived from it. He radiated protection. It had been far too long since anyone had felt protective toward her.

Tess breathed a little easier when they reached the relative safety of Nate's apartment. She focused on the food, clearing the coffee table and rooting around in his kitchen for a couple of plates.

"Do you want silverware, or just the chopsticks?"

He didn't answer her. She found him standing at the window, staring down into the street.

"Silverware or chopsticks?" she repeated.

"I'm gonna go talk to him," Nate said, never hearing her question.

"No! Nate, really, I don't think you should—"

"I know how to handle this," he said, shrugging

back into his jacket. "Stay here, lock the door behind me. I'll be back in five minutes with some answers."

Tess resisted the urge to fall on him, grab onto some body part, and try to keep him from going. She knew she wouldn't succeed. "Don't blame me if your food's cold when you get back," she said instead, pretending she didn't care.

Nate waited until the man's back was turned before he sauntered out the front door. He wanted the element of surprise on his side. The man turned casually back, then started. His eyes widened almost imperceptibly. He took an extra-long drag on his cigarette and threw it aside.

Nate strolled closer—within kicking distance. Unarmed, his only advantage should this confrontation get ugly was physical proximity. Martial arts weren't all that useful from twenty feet away.

But the man didn't reach for a weapon. He stood his ground, smiling nervously. " 'Evening."

"What do you want?" Nate asked without preamble.

"That's what I like, a man who gets right to the point. My name is Tristan Solca."

Nate took Solca's outstretched hand with no small amount of trepidation. "Nate Wagner."

"I apologize for alarming you and the woman last night. It was not my intention. I didn't realize how it would appear, a strange man coming out of the darkness—"

"You knew exactly how it would appear, or do you always go around making friends with a knife? You might have frightened Tess, but you don't scare me. What do you want?"

Any signs of civility vanished from Solca's face. "I want the Crimson Cat. It is mine, legally mine. Morganna gave it to me. It resided in my home for years, until I was burglarized. I finally traced it to Anne-Louise's shop, only to discover that this Judy Cosgrove had purchased it mere minutes before I got there."

Nate's stomach swooped. Tess had been right. Solca *was* after the Cat.

"What do I have to do with this?" Nate asked, feigning confusion. "Why aren't you talking to Judy?"

"Miss Cosgrove is in a hospital room, fighting for her life. Anyway, she no longer has possession of the Cat. You do. And I'm willing to buy it from you. I'll pay five hundred dollars."

Now Nate was baffled. How did this man know he and Tess had the statue? The thing had been wrapped in a bag when he'd carried it out of Judy's apartment. He couldn't help but voice the question. "How do you know—"

"I felt it," Solca said. "This is something you, with your white Anglo-Saxon Protestant upbringing, will never understand, but I have a spiritual connection to the statue. I need it. It completes me."

This was too weird. What if all that stuff Tess had spouted about Gypsies wielding the Cat's power for evil purposes . . . no. It was ridiculous even to consider. Still, he had to ask, "Are you by any chance de-scended from Gypsies?"

Solca's face hardened. "I am from Romania. What has that to do with anything?"

"You're the one who brought up the differences be-tween us."

"Enough of this," Solca said, spitting. "Are you go-ing to sell me the statue or not?"

"I can't," Nate replied. There was nothing he would like better than to rid himself of the thing. He could turn the considerable profit over to Judy, for whom it might come in handy. Hospital stays weren't cheap, even for those with good insurance.

But Tess would be livid, not to mention frightened to pieces, if he sold the statue to someone she believed would use it for evil purposes. She was intent on cast-ing this ridiculous spell.

Maybe a compromise would work. "We'll be done with the statue in a few days. After that, I might per-suade Tess to part with it."

Solca narrowed his gaze. "What are you planning to do with it during this 'few days'?"

"Nothing I can talk about." And still sound sane.

"The spell! Damn, I should have known the witch's little daughter would try to succeed where her mother had failed. Fools! Don't you know that's what drove Morganna insane? The Cat's powers aren't to be taken lightly. Moonbeam will only succeed in hurting her-self."

Nate refused to be drawn into this group delusion. He was willing to admit that Tess had abilities—maybe everyone had them. But the Crimson Cat was just a statue, made of stone. It didn't have powers.

"Believe what you will," he said. "The Cat is not for sale at this time." He folded his arms and stood implacably before Solca. "If you don't stop hanging around in front of my building, I'll call the police. Do I make myself clear?"

"Perfectly." Solca reached inside his tweed jacket and Nate stiffened, ready for anything. But all he withdrew was a business card. "Call me if you change your mind. If you're still able to dial a phone when the Cat is done with you."

Tess had watched the exchange from the window. Nothing seemed out of the ordinary about it. Two men standing on the sidewalk, talking. It was over in less than three minutes.

She rushed to the door and unlocked it when she heard Nate's footsteps on the landing. She swung the door wide. "What happened?"

He stood there with key in hand. "Tess, the reason I had you lock the door is so no one could get in. How did you know it was me out here?"

"I knew," she said with certainty.

Nate sighed, lowered the key, and walked in. "His name is Tristan Solca. He's Romanian, which means he could have Gypsy blood. He wants the Cat. He claims your mother gave it to him, and it was subsequently stolen."

"What did you tell him?"

"That it wasn't for sale. Not even for five hundred dollars." He shook his head, appearing mystified. "I must be crazy."

Tess drooped with relief. "You did the right thing."

"Would you be interested in selling it after we remove the curse?" he asked in a conversational tone, as if removing a curse were as easy as taking out a grass stain from a favorite pair of jeans.

"Let's just take this one step at a time," Tess said. "And the next step is food. It's getting cold."

They fell on the Chinese food. Tess was hungrier than she could ever remember being. She inhaled her vegetables and rice, fried wonton, and spring roll, savoring every flavor. Like a doomed prisoner enjoying a final meal, she couldn't help thinking. They ate without talking much, other than an occasional "Pass the soy sauce."

The food was gone in record time. Nate cleared the dishes and loaded them into the dishwasher; Tess gathered the paper cartons and trashed them, then wiped down the coffee table. Each move she made brought her closer to that inevitable moment when she would have to face the grimoire and the spell. Her powers, such as they were, would be called into battle.

Was she strong enough? Was she worthy? Morganna had once claimed that Tess had more natural ability, more potential, than any witch she'd ever known, including herself. But without training and practice, Tess's gifts were little more than untried mettle.

"Well, let's get cracking," Nate said, rubbing his

hands together. "Should I light a candle or some-thing?"

She shot him a long-suffering look. Should she tell him she'd once seen her mother grow a flower from a seed in five minutes, using a spell from this very book? No. Why bother? He'd be a believer soon enough.

"I would appreciate it if you would handle the book," she said. "Even after all these years the thing reeks of my mother's vibrations, and I find that dis-tracting."

He shrugged. "Sure." Then he grabbed up the book as if it were a football instead of a fragile, hun-dred-year-old volume, and plopped it onto the coffee table. "I'm more comfortable on the floor. How about you?"

In the end, she was the one who sat on the floor with the book before her on the coffee table. Nate sat in the chair behind her, straddling her with his knees, reaching over her to turn the pages so they could both see. Tess had procured pen and paper for writing down the ingredients they would need to collect.

"I lost my place when we had the wreck," Nate said as he nonchalantly turned pages, "but I think I can find it again—wait, here it is." He pressed the book flat, smoothing out the creased and wrinkled page. The binding protested with a crack.

Tess stared at the page, yellowed with age, the let-ters executed in a flawless calligraphic script. It wasn't Morganna's more flamboyant handwriting, but proba-bly that of Tess's grandmother.

" 'A Spell to Counteract Black Magick,' " Tess read

aloud. " 'If thou be cursed or hexed by thine enemy, work thee this spell to break the bonds of evil.' "

"Where's Vincent Price?" Nate muttered. "He ought to be here for this."

Tess ignored him and went on. " 'Heed thee this warning: The powers summoned for this spell are not of this world. Use it only in the direst circumstances. Prepare thyself and take caution; deviate not from the proscription here, not in the smallest detail, at the risk of peril to thine immortal soul.' "

Tess shivered. Nate snorted. "What, exactly, is that supposed to mean?"

"I think it means that this isn't exactly white magic. But I already knew that. Any spell that can backfire and hurt you is bad stuff."

"It's not going to hurt us," Nate said. "It's like voodoo. It can only do us harm if we believe in it."

"I *do* believe in it."

"We have the purest of intentions," he tried again, leaning closer. His breath disturbed her hair and tickled her ear. "We're not seeking vengeance, or trying to hurt anybody else."

"But we'll be asking help from the wrong sort."

"Then let's not ask them," he said, as if the answer were obvious. "Isn't there some other 'sort' we can call for assistance? How about . . . I don't know. Angels? Saints?"

"I'm afraid those are outside my frame of reference. Look, if you'd rather not go through with this—"

He shook his head. "You're the one afraid of evil,

not me. I'm game. Let's follow the spell to the letter and see what happens."

She nodded in agreement. Then she read further, and was seized with all kinds of doubts again. "This has to be performed during a full moon. That's tomorrow night."

"Ah, so that's what Morganna meant. She said something about the moon as we were leaving. That's okay. We can do it. The sooner the better, right?"

"At midnight. In a churchyard. At the grave of one who died a violent death."

Nate suddenly ran out of glib comebacks. "Did you say a churchyard? Is that like . . . a cemetery?"

"Yes."

"Hoo, boy," he said under his breath. "Is that the worst of it?" He peered over her shoulder. "Holy cow, look at that list of ingredients."

Tess almost smiled. She was familiar with most of the components of the spell, but to Nate, the list had to seem like some twisted version of a Julia Child recipe— one of those ones you watch on TV but could never make at home because you have no idea where to find pigeon livers or variegated couscous.

"A white candle and garlic powder I can probably manage," Nate said, "but where are we supposed to get unhexing oil? Dried and powdered sloe bark? Agrimony? I don't even know what that stuff is."

"Agrimony? It's an herb, in the rose family." She wondered at her knowledge. Maybe some of Morganna's teachings had sunk in despite Tess's best efforts. "We can find most of the ingredients in an occult shop," she said calmly. "I think there's one right here in Cambridge."

She turned the page. The list of ingredients continued.

"Green ash-tree leaves. Do we even have ash trees in Boston?" Nate groused. "And what about *that*? Oh, hell, we're toast. The *blood of a virgin*? Yeah, right. Where are we supposed to come up with something like that?"

Tess stayed very quiet. She could easily alleviate Nate's apprehensions about finding that particular ingredient, but she didn't think she could bear to tell him *she* was a virgin. It seemed so pathetic to be twenty-eight and without any sexual experience at all.

"Well?" he said. "We're supposed to grab some fifteen-year-old from a convent school and bleed her? I mean, in this day and age you just don't find virgins on every corner. Maybe it was an easier proposition at the time this spell was written—"

"Enough, already!" Tess broke in. "We'll find a virgin's blood, okay? Trust me on this one."

"You know someone who would actually donate their daughter's blood to this craziness? 'Cause I'm telling you, I'm not doing it without parental consent. I don't need a jail term."

Now Tess was hot. "You assume there aren't any virgins above the age of consent in all of Boston?"

"Well, there might be a nun or two," Nate said.

"And I guess all the rest are just panting to go to bed with you or anyone who'll take them? You've never heard of celibacy?" She was really pushing it here. The fact was, she was a virgin not because of any lofty moral codes, but because she'd never found a practical way to change her status.

"Let me put it this way," Nate said. "I hear celibacy bandied about, but I don't know any virgins."

"Yes, you do," Tess said, exasperated.

"No, really, I don't think—"

"Me, you idiot. *I'm* the virgin." In a quieter voice, she added, "We can use my blood."

Nate was dumbstruck. How could he have been so stupid, so ignorant? Tess had told him often enough how uncomfortable touching was for her, but he'd assumed, on some level, that she was exaggerating.

"How old are you? Twenty-seven?"

"Twenty-eight. Don't rub it in."

"Sorry. It's just that . . . well, I'm only a few years older than you, and sex is one of my greatest pleasures. No, it's *the* greatest pleasure, has been since I was seventeen. Call me shallow, if you will." And just talking about it was making him hard. Tess, a virgin.

He'd thought about making love to her, maybe only a million times since he'd met her. Now, knowing what he knew, he had to ask himself what were the chances?

"Pretty damn slim at the moment," she quipped.

"Ahhhhghrmn!" Nate jumped away from her. "You read my mind."

"I told you I could do that on occasion," she said mildly.

"I knew you could get vibrations from objects, but . . . it doesn't seem fair, somehow. You . . . turn around so I can at least look at you?"

She did as he asked, swiveling in the space in front of his chair and curling her legs under her. "You see the problem?"

"Huh, yeah." What man would want a woman knowing every single thought that crossed his mind when he was making love to her? Like, what if some guy mentally compared her to his last girlfriend? Not that Nate would do that. Or, what if, while some guy was caressing her breasts, he wondered what she might look like with silicone implants? Instant slap. Not that Nate would ever think that, either. He thought Tess's breasts were perfect.

A sudden thought occurred to him. "Can you read my mind right now?"

She shook her head. "Not unless we're touching, and even then, not a hundred percent. If it makes you feel any better, I've read your mind quite a bit over the last few days—"

"Oh, yeah, feeling better already." What had he thought? What did she know about him?

"—and," she continued doggedly, "I haven't picked up one single thing that made me uncomfortable. That's a first. In fact, I'd even started to think . . . well, that maybe you could be the one who, um . . ." She stopped, unable to continue, as her face turned a becoming shade of pink.

Was she saying what he thought she was saying?

Suddenly everything changed. "God, Tess, I'd be,

you know, honored and—" No, that wasn't what he wanted to say. "Thrilled. Real happy to be—I could give it a try. Of course, if you knew what I was thinking the whole time . . . well, I'm a guy. Guys think all kinds of things different from women, but we don't mean anything by it."

"I understand," Tess said. Then she flashed a shy smile that undid him.

He couldn't stand it. He had to touch her. She knew what he was thinking anyway, he figured. He was one big mass of quivering hormones right now, and all he wanted was to be closer, closer. He reached for her.

She didn't flinch or pull away. In fact, she leaned in when he grasped her under her arms and pulled her gently into his lap. She was so light, so soft, and she smelled like something rare and fleeting.

He cradled her face between his hands and brought her lips to his. She tasted faintly salty, then so sweet. His mind filled with all sorts of sensual images that he was helpless to stop, so he didn't even try.

"Mm-hmm," she murmured against his mouth as her arms stole around his neck. "Oh, yes."

Was she sharing his thoughts, or just approving of the way he rubbed her back?

"Both," she whispered.

He was just reaching his stride with the kiss when abruptly she tensed and pulled away a short distance, staring intently into his eyes. "Oh, my God, it's going to happen."

"Good," was all Nate could think to say. If he

didn't have this woman in the next ten minutes, he was going to explode.

"I've been seeing flashes of this ever since I first held your business card, but I wasn't sure—"

"I'm sure," he said, cutting her off with another kiss. He'd been seeing flashes, too, and he wasn't psychic. His hands wandered away from her back to her front, lingering on just the sides of her breasts, not wanting to move too quickly. Oh, yes, they were the perfect size, just right to rest in a man's palms. Slowly he brought his thumbs to her nipples and gave a groan of satisfaction when they hardened.

Suddenly she tensed again, pushed him away, and scrambled to her feet as if he had the plague. The look of horror on her face was alarming.

"Tess?"

"We can't do this! I'm a virgin!"

Nate felt cold and abandoned and none too rational. "It's not a terminal condition."

"The spell." She lowered her voice to a more rational tone. "I can't compromise my status as a virgin until we've cast the spell."

The spell. The Cat. Right now he wished he could throw the grimoire and that infernal statue into a cement mixer and be done with it. But he could tell, just by the hard glint in Tess's eyes, that she wouldn't be swayed on this particular point. Whatever he and Tess might be headed for, it wasn't going to happen tonight.

NINE

Only one ingredient for the spell remained to be discussed. Tess read of it silently. She knew Nate did too. "The blood of a virgin, *and a lock of hair from her own true love.*" Neither of them said a word about it. It simply wasn't mentioned.

Tess had never been in love. She'd never even known anyone involved in a lifelong, monogamous, loving relationship. Her father had died before she knew him, and Morganna spoke little of him, leading Tess to believe her parents hadn't truly been in love. Morganna had been involved in a few other relationships over the years, but none of them had lasted longer than a few months.

True love was harder to find than virgin's blood, in Tess's opinion. The spell was doomed to failure. Yet she felt compelled to push forward. Maybe something would occur to them, some way to make an exception or get around the dictates of the spell. Or maybe they would stumble upon another virgin, one who had a boyfriend, at least.

Right.

"I think we should get started tonight," she said. "The occult shop might still be open. And we can start checking out cemeteries."

Nate tugged at his collar, which was already loose. "Mmm."

She felt silly asking her next question, but they had to start somewhere. "Do you know of anyone who died a violent death?"

He pondered for a moment. "I can think of a couple of people. But, Tess, we can't expect to hang out at a cemetery in the middle of the night, doing weird things. The police will haul us in. We'll have to find some place out of the city."

They fell silent for a few more moments.

"Wait, I know," Tess said. "A girl in my high school died in a car accident. That counts as violent, right?"

"I'd say so."

"She was buried in this little graveyard at a church in Sudbury. The whole school turned out for the funeral, including me."

"You remember where it is?"

She shrugged. "Sure. Sudbury's not that big. Unless you can come up with a better idea. Let's do the occult shop first, though."

Nate wholeheartedly agreed with that suggestion.

Tess found the shop in the Yellow Pages. It was only

a few blocks away, on Inman Square, and it was open till nine on Tuesdays. They decided to walk.

Inman Square was lively, the eclectic mixture of trendy nightspots and eccentric little shops drawing students, young professionals, and older, longtime residents. It was a pleasant night, so the streets were busy. Soft saxophone music rolled out of one of the clubs as the door opened to admit a scruffy group of students. A rare-book store had a lively sidewalk sale going on. Laundry hung in the alleys tucked away behind fashionable restaurants.

Nate spotted the occult shop first. "Over there, in that corner. That's it."

Tess squinted in the direction he pointed. The Dragon's Lair. She could just make out the letters on the old-fashioned sign, which was supposed to be shaped like a dragon, but which looked more like a friendly salamander to Tess. She stepped off the curb toward it.

She felt the hot breath of the approaching car before she saw it. In the same instant she sensed danger, she was jerked backward by the arm so hard that she stumbled and fell onto the curb, bruising her elbow. A huge black Lincoln Continental roared past unapologetically, missing Tess's foot by centimeters.

Nate dropped down beside her. "Tess, you okay? Tess?"

She was surprised and dazed, but that was all. "I think so."

"The nerve of that jerk," Nate muttered. "He didn't even stop. You could have been killed!"

A small crowd of concerned bystanders had gathered around Tess. She allowed Nate to help her to her feet and brush her off. Her elbow throbbed, but it was probably just a bruise. "I'm fine, really," she assured everyone.

"He didn't even have his lights on," someone commented.

"Came out of nowhere," someone else said.

Nate put his arm protectively around Tess. "Sure you're okay?"

She nodded. "Let's go. I'm not letting anything stop me now. The curse will have to kill me if it wants to prevent this spell from being cast."

"It damn near did!" But he continued with her to the occult shop. He was quiet, thoughtful. Maybe he was wondering if there wasn't something to this curse stuff after all.

That was good, Tess decided. She wanted the full power of his belief behind her—along with his fear, and his desire to conquer the curse.

Many years had passed since she had entered an occult shop. Her mother had dragged her to more than a few when she'd been a little girl, though. This particular one had a warm, friendly feel about it—nothing overtly geared toward black magic. No skulls or bats or voodoo charms, or any of the other nonsense that sometimes graced the hokier shops.

Nate and Tess were the only customers. A large, round, earth-mother type greeted them from behind the counter. She had long, frizzy hair halfway down her back and a wreath of flowers on her head.

Tess pulled the shopping list from her pocket. "Hi. Maybe it would be faster if I just gave you this?"

"Certainly," the woman said, adjusting her wire-rim glasses to peer at the crumpled piece of paper. "Hmm."

"You have most of those things, right?" Tess asked anxiously.

"Well, yes. All but the ash leaves. I'm out of those. But I can tell you where an ash tree grows." She continued to frown at the list, making no move to fetch the ingredients.

"I'll also need a chalice, an athame, and a censer of some kind," Tess said, hoping to prompt the woman into action.

At that request, the woman looked up sharply. "You don't already have those things? Not that it's any of my business, but any witch worth her sea salt would recognize that these are ingredients for a spell to counteract black magic. A complicated ritual, given the length of the list. Please don't tell me this is the first spell you've ever tried to cast."

"I studied the Old Religion from my mother's knee," Tess hedged. "I've been out of it for a while, so I'm rusty, but not a rank beginner."

The woman looked relieved. "Well, okay then. I'll just gather these things up for you." She grabbed a straw basket from behind the counter and began poking around in various jars and drawers, humming tunelessly.

Tess leaned against the scarred oak counter. She was suddenly unbearably tired, and her elbow throbbed. She flexed it a couple of times, hoping to prevent it from getting stiff. Then she chanced a look at Nate, who had been unusually quiet ever since their encounter with the Continental.

He wasn't looking at her. He was staring toward the floor, several feet away.

Tess followed his gaze. There crouched a skinny Siamese cat, teeth bared, tail switching.

"It's growling at me." Nate barely breathed the words. "Hear that low rumble? What is the deal here? Animals normally like me."

Tess didn't bother to answer the question. Wasn't it obvious to him what was going on? Cats were highly intuitive creatures. That was why witches for centuries had been choosing them for their familiars. This cat, like Judy's, sensed the vibration of the curse.

The shop's proprietress returned to the counter, her basket filled with plastic bags and tiny glass vials containing various powders, crushed herbs and flower petals, and exotically colored liquids. Just as she opened her mouth to speak, the cat hissed, issued an earsplitting yowl, and streaked for the back of the shop.

"That is so strange," she said, staring after her retreating pet. "He's normally the sweetest cat, loves everybody." With a shrug she pulled out a receipt book and started writing up the purchases. Nate paid for them without a word, casting a wary glance now and then as if watching for the cat to reappear.

The woman gave them directions to the ash grove, which was right in the Boston Common, and they walked back out into the cool night.

"What next?" Tess asked, injecting a note of lightheartedness she did not feel into her voice. "The ash grove, or the cemetery?"

"Ash grove," Nate answered immediately. "I say we postpone the cemetery until tomorrow morning. It'll be a lot harder to find the grave we're searching for in the dark."

"Okay," Tess agreed. She wasn't really looking forward to the graveyard, but she hadn't wanted to be a baby about it. Apparently Nate wasn't all that eager to visit such a grim place at night, either. They would have to face it tomorrow night, of course. But tomorrow night, she was determined to squelch all fear.

"I know it's getting late," Tess ventured as they strode determinedly back toward Nate's apartment, "but could we squeeze in a visit to Judy? I don't want her to think we've abandoned her. I'll go by myself if you'd rather not."

"You're not going anywhere without me. Not with that nut Tristan Solca still out there somewhere, and strange Lincolns trying to run you down."

She didn't argue with him. It made her feel warm from the inside out to know that Nate worried about her safety.

"We can take the T," he said. "Then we don't have to worry about parking."

Or car accidents, Tess added silently. Or running out of gas, or engine problems or flat tires. All in all, the T did seem the safer way to go.

That was before the power went out on the subway, leaving them stranded in a tunnel in a dark, dead train.

Tess couldn't help it. She screamed—not a blood-curdling horror-movie scream, but something between a yelp and a shriek.

Nate's arm immediately went around her. "It's okay, Tess. It's just a power outage."

"This doesn't happen during a normal power outage," she pointed out. "They have backup generators for that kind of thing."

"Then maybe there was an accident—a derailment or something. I'm sure it'll start up again soon."

Fortunately the car wasn't crowded. Those few passengers who were there grumbled uneasily, but no one panicked.

"What if *we* did this?" Tess whispered. "What if the curse caused a subway car to derail? What if people are killed?"

"Just because we decided to ride the T? Tess, be reasonable. I know you believe the curse is powerful, but if it could kill people indiscriminately, people who have no connection with the Cat statue, then we ought to notify the Pentagon. It's the best weapon since the Ark of the Covenant."

He was right, Tess told herself. She needed to calm down. She took several slow, deep breaths, but only succeeded in convincing herself that without the ventilation system, the car was running out of oxygen. "I still think this is no coincidence. The Cat is trying to slow us down, prevent us from casting the spell—ow!"

"What?"

"Someone bumped into me and stepped on my—my purse!"

"Someone stepped on your purse?"

"No, they stepped on my toe and stole my purse." She felt all around her, hoping she was mistaken, but her vinyl bag was nowhere around.

Just then the lights flickered back on and the car lurched forward. She looked around at the other passengers accusingly. None would meet her eye.

"There," Nate said, pointing to the aisle. Her bag lay open on the floor, its contents spilling out. "Maybe you just dropped it."

Tess stepped out of her seat to retrieve the purse, scooping the contents back inside. Her billfold was open, she noticed. Checking it, she found all of her cash gone.

"No, I was robbed." She cast withering glares at the other passengers, hoping she would shame the guilty party into returning the fifty or sixty bucks she'd lost. They all ignored her.

"Hell," Nate muttered. "What else can happen?"

"Don't ask."

Nate wanted very badly not to believe in curses. But their luck went from bad to worse. Tess twisted her ankle when they got off at the Charles Street/Mass General T-stop. She limped the two blocks to the hospital but insisted they didn't have time to waste with medical treatment for a minor injury.

When they arrived on Judy's floor, things went from worse to wretched. Judy's condition had been downgraded from serious to critical. She had dropped into a coma.

"But she could still be okay, right?" Tess asked, almost desperately.

The doctor who'd been kind enough to fill them in shook his head pessimistically. "Once this syndrome advances to this stage, the prognosis is very bad. I can tell you that she's comfortable, but her vital signs are gradually growing weaker."

Tess's eyes filled and her lower lip trembled. "H-how long does she have?"

The doctor shrugged. "I don't have that answer."

Tess's eyes flashed with sudden intensity. "Until tomorrow night. You have to keep her alive until tomorrow night. Is that possible?"

"Again, I don't know."

As soon as Judy's parents took a break from visiting their daughter in ICU, Tess and Nate were allowed a brief visit. Nate was shocked at how much Judy's appearance had deteriorated since the day before. It seemed that her cheeks were hollower, her skin and hair duller. And she was so still.

"Listen to me, Judy," Tess whispered urgently as she leaned close to the fragile-looking form in the bed, though she touched nothing. "You hang on until tomorrow night. We're going to fix it for you. Right after midnight, I promise, you'll start feeling better."

She looked up at Nate. "Say something to her. I know she can hear us."

On the spot, Nate stumbled through a quick, insincere speech. But he finished up with a sentiment that was a hundred-percent truthful. "Judy, I don't know you very well, but you strike me as a fighter. Now's the time to fight, kiddo. Hang in there for Tess." His words came out thick. He had to swallow back the lump in his throat.

"That was really good, Nate. Thanks."

"Well, I try. Do you think you could . . . I mean, what would happen if you touched her?"

Tess shook her head. "I don't want to. I'm afraid I would feel . . . nothing." Her eyes teared up again.

Nate longed to reach for Tess, to comfort her. But by now he knew enough that his touch was anything but comforting to her. He didn't want to add to her ordeal.

Then she surprised him. For the first time she reached for him. She sought his embrace. He welcomed her into the shelter of his arms and let her cry against his shoulder.

A nurse hustled them out of ICU. They met with Judy's parents briefly, offering a few encouraging words, then escaped into the cool, dark night.

The Public Garden, where the ash trees were purported to grow, was only a short walk from the hospital. Actually locating the grove among the fifty-plus species of trees growing there, however, was more of a challenge. When Nate finally spotted it, the grove of four trees was enclosed by a little fence that fairly shouted "Do Not Touch."

But Nate wasn't about to waste the opportunity. "Wait for me here."

"Nate, you can't—"

He was over the fence in seconds. He tore his jacket on one of the spikes, then disturbed a pair of snoozing geese, which had the gall to chase him a few strides before waddling away.

The trees were tall and spindly. Nate looked up. "Aw, hell." No way to reach any leaves without climbing. Even the ground beneath the trees was recently raked. With a sigh, he did his best imitation of a monkey, hugging the trunk with his feet and knees, inching his way upward to the lowest branch.

He heard Tess whisper something urgently from the fence, but he couldn't quite make out the words. From his precarious perch, he searched frantically for her. Was she in trouble? The park was deserted this time of night.

All at once he was blinded by a flashlight beam in the face. "And what would you be doing up there, Tarzan?" a husky, very unfriendly voice asked. Figuring this was his last chance, he grabbed a handful of leaves and crammed them into his pocket before swinging down from the tree.

"Uh, evening, Officer." The uniformed patrolman he faced was at least six-four and a solid wall of muscle. Tess stood trembling beside him.

"You're trespassing. Destroying public property."

"Yes, well, I know, but I didn't intend any harm."

"What were you doing up there?" the officer asked.

"He was gathering some leaves from the ash tree," Tess broke in. "For me. These are the only ash trees we know of in the area."

"And what do you need them for?"

"A, um, botany project," Nate interrupted. If Tess started spouting anything about spells or magic, the cop would haul them in for sure. "She's a student, and she has this big project due tomorrow." It wasn't exactly a lie.

Tess's eyes widened, but she didn't contradict him.

The cop rolled his eyes. "Why don't you college kids stay in Cambridge where you belong? All right, get out of here, the both of you. Since it's near the end of my shift, I'll let you off."

"Thank you," they said together. Then they scurried away before he changed his mind. Nate's breathing didn't return to normal until they were riding the ancient wooden escalator down to the Park Street T Station.

Tess stood stiff and tense next to him as they stepped onto the subway car. The lights flickered, as if the Crimson Cat were reminding them that it hadn't forgotten about them. Nate had to resist the urge to jump back off the car before the doors closed.

"Did you see that?" Tess asked, clinging to him.

"Yeah." He stifled a tremor.

"I feel like the curse is toying with us, letting us know that it could stop us any time. For good."

It's just coincidence, Nate said to himself. A long, serious streak of bad luck. Nothing more. He breathed a huge sigh of relief when they made it home alive. At least they hadn't seen any more of Tristan Solca.

Tess didn't make even a token suggestion that she should go home, for which Nate was glad. He didn't want to spend the night alone any more than he imagined Tess wanted to, and he certainly didn't want to venture out again to see her home. By silent agreement he helped her fold out the sofa bed. He gave her an old football jersey to sleep in. It covered her much too decently, all the way to her mid-thigh, except he thought he could see the shadows of her nipples through the pin-sized holes that peppered the jersey fabric.

He tried not to stare as they settled at the dining table with cups of hot chocolate.

"I'm scared," she said. They'd avoided talking about anything consequential since the subway. "I hope you're not. You seem so solid, so unflappable, and that's a comfort to me."

"No, I'm not scared. Apprehensive, maybe." Worried about the toll all this magic preparation was taking on Tess. Dark circles marred the translucent skin beneath her eyes. She'd hardly eaten all day.

And she trembled. Like a little bird, or a frightened puppy.

He was worried about Judy. Hell, he hardly knew the woman, but he felt unaccountably close to her anyway, because of his involvement with Tess. He worried about how Tess would react if the spell didn't work, if they lost Judy despite their heroic efforts.

And, okay, he was just the tiniest bit worried that he would have to live the rest of his life—however brief that might be—shadowed by a curse.

"I know I need to sleep," Tess said, "to gather my strength, but I'm not sure I can."

"I'll stay with you if you want," he offered, knowing full well that if he lay next to Tess, *he* would be the one who didn't get any sleep.

"Oh, no, I didn't mean—that is, I'm sure you wouldn't want to—"

"You'd be safe. Much as I want to make love to you, I'm taking this virgin thing pretty seriously."

The color flooding her cheeks only reminded him how pale she was looking without the blush.

"It's your call," he said, reaching across the table to lay his hands over hers. "If you'd rather I keep my distance, I'll be in the next room."

"One scream away." Her grim smile faded almost as soon as it appeared. "I think we ought to stick together. Am I—would that be teasing you? To ask you to share my bed without any sex? Now you're finding out how naive I really am. I don't know the rules 'cause I've never played the games, but I know being a tease is bad."

"These are special circumstances," he said, wishing he had the strength to deny her request. But at this point he would do anything she asked of him. He was, he realized, completely nuts over the woman.

He was falling in love with a witch.

If Nate had any doubts about the efficacy of the curse, they were laid to rest the next morning. After a tense, eight-hour stretch of lying next to Tess and waking up from one nightmare after another, each more gruesome and terrifying than the last, he awoke to find that his hot-water heater had leaked to near empty during the night. Not only did he have to deal with a lake in his hallway, but he had to shower in ice water.

Then his toaster exploded when he tried to transform a couple of stale bagels into breakfast, causing a small fire in his kitchen. When he tried to pull the cord out of the wall socket, he damn near electrocuted himself.

If all that hadn't convinced him, the early-morning drive to Sudbury, where they planned to check out the cemetery, did. A tree fell on them, or very nearly so. Nate was driving Tess's car because of her swollen ankle, and a hundred-year-old tree suddenly heaved over for no apparent reason. Nate floored it, catching only the massive tree's outer branches on the back of the car.

He'd scarcely recovered from that fright when a drunk driver—or at least, someone who drove like a drunk—strayed across the center line of the highway and nearly front-ended them. Again, only Nate's quick reflexes and a mild flirtation with a ditch saved their lives. After those two near tragedies the curse didn't bother with staged accidents. The car itself tried to drive them off the road.

Nate held the steering wheel in a firm grip, using every muscle in his arms and shoulders to keep to his course.

"What's going on now?" Tess asked as she watched his struggle.

"The damn car seems to have a mind of its own. I can't—oh, God, no!" The car veered into oncoming traffic.

Tess grabbed the steering wheel; between them, amid honking and squealing tires, they narrowly avoided another collision.

"It's that next road, on the right," Tess said. "God, I can't believe this. Even the map has turned against us. I just got a paper cut that ought to have stitches!"

Nate followed her directions to the tiny church-yard, his stomach roiling. Why couldn't he wake up and find this whole trip was a continuation of the previous night's nightmares?

He pulled the car, obedient for the moment, under a huge chestnut tree and cut the motor.

"I *do* believe in curses," he chanted softly. "I do, I do, I do."

TEN

Tess thought Nate looked a little pale as he got out of the car, but she couldn't blame him. She was shaking herself. "You know," she said, "in a way, all these terrible things happening to us are a good sign."

Nate, who'd been rolling up the sleeves of his shirt, paused and looked at her. "Come again?"

"The curse, or whatever force is behind it, is working awfully hard at trying to stop us from casting the spell. That must mean we're on the right track. It must mean we have at least a chance of succeeding, or why would the Cat bother to stop us?"

Nate came and stood beside her. "I apologize."

"For what?"

"For not believing in this thing from the very beginning. I can't deny now that there is something very powerful out to get us."

"It's only natural for a logical person such as yourself to want proof."

"I have it now, that's for sure." His eyes bored into hers. "Tess, a minute ago you said 'the curse, or the force behind it.' What exactly are you talking about?"

Tess rubbed her upper arms, fighting off the chill that came from within. "I don't even want to speculate."

Her answer obviously didn't satisfy him, but he didn't press her, for which she was grateful. She'd already lain awake the night before thinking about the power of the force they were up against, speculating the worst. Morganna had mentioned something about a "Dark Lord."

She shivered again. "You ready?"

He nodded, his throat working as if he wanted to say something.

The cemetery was a small one, fenced in black wrought iron and nestled among some trees behind a picturesque white frame church—picture-postcard perfect. The area was deserted. They couldn't see anything around them but trees. It was a perfect setting for their midnight ritual.

The entry gate was locked, but the low fence didn't provide much of a deterrent. Even with her tender ankle, Tess didn't have much trouble vaulting the barricade. She waited for Nate to join her, but he didn't. She look back at him.

Nate stood on the outside looking in, his face frozen. He'd gone from pale to almost green.

"Nate? What's wrong?"

He swung his gaze toward her. "Remember that

first day we went out to the antique stores? And I accused you of having a phobia about cats?"

"Yeah . . ."

"I'm well acquainted with phobias. I have one."

"Cemeteries?" she squeaked. "That's right. You did say something about that. I remember now."

"Uh-huh. I thought—I mean, it's completely irrational. I know that. I intended to tough it out, but I don't seem to be able to make my legs take me over the fence. I can't even *look* at all those headstones without getting queasy."

"It's okay, Nate." She reached over the fence and touched his arm. Funny how automatic the gesture had become. Touching, which until a few days ago had been the bane of her existence, seemed completely natural with Nate. Comforting, even.

She felt his horror, though. Beads of perspiration popped out on her forehead and upper lip.

She nodded miserably, then shook herself. They had business to take care of, but there was no reason for them to linger in this place longer than necessary. "Stay here, Nate. You don't have to come inside the fence."

She turned and walked briskly toward the far corner of the cemetery, where the newer headstones were located. Vibrations reached out for her like grasping vines, but she determinedly shook them off. It took only a couple of minutes of scanning the epitaphs to locate Mary Beth Logan's headstone.

TAKEN TOO YOUNG, HER LIFE BARELY BEGUN, the etched granite stone read. SHE IS WITH THE ANGELS NOW.

A ribbon of grief laced itself through Tess's mind. She went with it for a moment, letting the tears come to her eyes, then released it. There, that wasn't so bad. She reached into the pocket of her jeans and pulled out a big white bow, which she stuck to the top of the headstone so they could easily locate the grave later that night.

It seemed almost too easy, she caught herself thinking as she hobbled on her sore ankle back toward the exit. But she supposed they were entitled to have *something* go right.

Nate waited for her exactly where she'd left him. He helped her over the fence. "Did you find it?"

"Yes."

He opened her car door for her, then walked around and folded himself behind the steering wheel. The car started right up and behaved perfectly as Nate pulled onto the road. Nothing more was said until the church and graveyard were well out of sight.

"I'm sorry," Nate said. "I feel like an idiot, a coward, to let a bunch of marble and granite and old bones scare me."

"Please don't apologize. Weren't you the one who told me not to be embarrassed about a phobia? That they were common?"

"Yeah, but that was before it was me acting irrationally." He paused, staring out the window. "My mother died when I was four."

Tess cringed inwardly. "Oh, Nate, that must have been horrible."

"I haven't been near a cemetery since, not even

when my sister died. But I thought I could . . . no, I will. I'll go in with you tonight, Tess. I promise. I stood there at the fence the whole time you were inside, and it wasn't as bad as I thought. I can do it."

"I know you can," she said simply, believing that with all her heart. Nate wasn't weak. He would do what needed to be done when the time came. She had absolute faith in him.

Everything was ready. Tess had assembled the ingredients for the spell and placed them in several canvas tote bags Nate had supplied. She had practiced reaching into the bags and withdrawing the various powders and whatnot in the order in which she would need them, assisted by her parapsychological powers. She had committed the spell itself to memory, then rehearsed it at least a hundred times, so that she could chant the appropriate words at the right moment without stumbling.

She had coached Nate on his responsibilities, which he was suddenly taking very seriously.

Finally she had taken a ritual bath in cool water laced with sea salt. Nate made them some potato soup and peanut-butter sandwiches for dinner, but Tess could hardly touch the food. Her stomach was tied in knots no Boy Scout ever knew. She meditated, using some long-ago-learned mantra, trying to make herself calm and serene. The potential for mistakes was huge, and she didn't want nerves to be a contributing factor.

After dinner, she called the hospital. Judy's condition had deteriorated further. "Now would be the time to come," the nurse whispered confidentially.

Oh, God, what a choice to have to make, she thought as she woodenly hung up the phone. Should she go to her friend and be with her during her final hours, or should she risk everything with a dangerous magic ritual?

Nate took her hand. "We have to do the spell," he said. "I know you want to be with her, but if we don't finish this thing, I'm afraid we'll all be seeing each other sooner than we like—on some other plane, if you get my drift."

She knew exactly what he was talking about, and she was forced to agree with him. "Nate, do you realize you just read my mind? I was thinking about the choice I had to make, and you responded as if I'd posed the question out loud."

Nate looked confused. "You *did* say it out loud."

She shook her head, looking down pointedly at their hands, which they'd unconsciously joined. "Maybe the connection goes two ways?"

He shook his head. "I'm not psychic."

"Everyone's psychic to some degree," she said, but with that she let the matter drop. The idea intrigued her, though. No one had ever picked up *her* vibrations before.

By nine-thirty, she felt ready. She figured they had at least an hour, though, before they needed to leave for the cemetery. An hour before they took the final, irreversible steps in this macabre drama.

They sat in the living room, each of them in one of

the club chairs, staring at each other. Tess had noticed that Nate had started avoiding the leather couch, the way she did. She wondered why.

"You can back out now if you want," she said suddenly. "I can do it alone."

He shook his head. "No way. I started this thing with you, and I'm going to finish it."

"One or both of us might be killed," she said, just in case he hadn't figured that out.

He had. "I know that. I believe it. But we've already cheated death more than once, even if it was by inches. I have to believe we'll keep cheating the bastard."

They fell silent for a time. Tess became more aware of the darkness outside. She knew the exact moment that the moon rose above the horizon—she could feel the rays of pale light enhancing her power. Her blood seemed to race through her veins. Her skin became almost unbearably sensitive, so that she was aware of every fiber of her clothing rubbing against her.

Or, she considered, maybe the way she felt had nothing to do with magic, other than the ordinary man-woman kind. Nate's gaze was trained on her, palpable as a caress. She suddenly remembered how it had felt to kiss him, to have his arms around her. Her body reacted to the memory, sending a surge of warmth to her center.

"Nate."

"Yes?"

"If I . . ." She stopped, choosing her words very carefully. "If we don't succeed in lifting the curse, I don't know what will become of us—death, insanity, or just miserable bad luck for the rest of our lives."

"Yeah. We've covered that ground."

"Well, I don't want to go to my fate without knowing . . . what it's like . . . to be loved." Her face flushed hot. She couldn't believe what she was about to suggest. But impending doom had turned her brazen.

Nate's eyes widened. "I thought you couldn't. You have to—I mean—" He sputtered to a stop. "What do you mean?"

"We can't physically make love," she said hastily, determined now to voice her idea. "But we've developed a pretty strong psychic link. If you were to hold me and—and *think* about what we would do if we could . . ." Oh, was this an idiotic idea or what?

Nate appeared truly stunned at first, but then a slow smile spread across his face. "I'm not sure you want to know what I'm thinking. It's pretty strong stuff."

"Yes, I do," she said with as much conviction as she could muster. "I want to be one with you, body and soul. If we can't do the body thing right now, then I want to see into your soul."

"But I won't be able to see into yours," he said, his voice like black velvet against her senses. Just the same he rose from his chair and came toward her. He drew very close, but he didn't touch her.

"If you open yourself up, maybe you can," she said. "You already read my mind once. And you've stopped sitting on the leather sofa, like maybe you have a little part of me in you already."

He looked over at the sofa, his face reflecting amazement. "I *have* been avoiding it."

She held her hand out to him. "Touch me, Nate. Please?"

Slowly his large hand enfolded hers, warm and reassuring. "You didn't honestly think I was going to refuse, did you?" He pulled her to her feet, then encircled her lightly with his arms. "Like this?"

"Mmm." She leaned her head against his shoulder. Already his vibrations were nudging her consciousness. Rather than tensing up, she relaxed against him and opened her mind. This was Nate. Whatever he was thinking about her—no matter how earthy it might be—would never hurt her.

Nate ran his hands up and down her back, relaxing her further. "I don't know about you," he murmured against her hair, "but I think we ought to sit down for this. Otherwise we might injure ourselves."

She leaned into him. He almost made her smile. "Your fantasies are that good, huh?"

"Wait and see." He maneuvered himself into the chair she'd just vacated, then pulled her into his lap. "Lean back and put your head on my shoulder. I'll just put my arms around you like this. . . ."

There were no more words, at least not that Tess was aware of. She closed her eyes, took a deep breath, and let the images come to her.

She found herself in a room surrounded by white satin drapes. She wore a flowing gauzy dress, her bare feet sinking into plush carpeting. In the center of the room was a mound of silk-covered pillows in all shades of pastel. She could smell the delicate scent of roses.

She had only a moment to appreciate the decadence of her environment, when Nate appeared beside her. He looked much as he did in real life, wearing worn jeans and a crisp cotton shirt, but the wild glint of passion in his eyes, unchecked, was something new. A thrill coursed through her, followed by liquid heat. She'd had no idea a man's eyes could be so arousing.

He touched her arm lightly and paused, as if asking for permission to continue. But when she looked up into his face looming above her, those passion-shined, determined eyes, she knew nothing in the world would stop this fantasy. She couldn't even open her eyes and put a halt to things—as if she wanted to. Her physical body was paralyzed.

Her fantasy body was anything but, yet she found that her free will had little to do with how the fantasy played out. She moved as he wanted her to, though without his saying a word.

It seemed perfectly natural to turn away from him and allow him to unfasten the long row of tiny buttons down her back. She shivered with pleasure each time his fingers came in contact with her bare skin as he accomplished the task quickly and smoothly.

When he was finished, the gauze dress slid off her shoulders and down to pool at her feet. To her surprise, though not her displeasure, she was completely bare underneath it.

She was not embarrassed in the least to have Nate see her this way. Of course, why would she be? It was a dream. But it felt like so much more than a dream, as if their souls were commingling on some astral plane. It felt more real than any vision she'd ever experienced.

Nate continued to stand behind her, his hands on her shoulders, nuzzling her sensitive nape. "You're so beautiful," he murmured. His breath was warm against her skin, and she found herself wishing he would move those strong-but-sensitive hands of his to other places on her body, the places that tingled with longing.

She wondered idly how she looked in his mind, then realized that he couldn't see her. He might be using his imagination to dream up this fantasy, but she alone was experiencing it. That thought made her a little sad.

Immersing herself in the experience soon overshadowed any melancholy thoughts. She bathed in the glow of his approval as he ran his hands lightly along her back, exploring each muscle as if he were playing doctor, rubbing his thumbs along her spine. He cupped her buttocks briefly, causing her heart to try to beat its way out of her chest.

Then he whirled her around to face him.

He was naked. How he got that way, she supposed, was no concern of hers. She breathed in and out, taking in the sight of his beautiful body with its tanned, hard planes. The hair on his chest, just a light dusting, was light brown with a surprising tawny glint to it. His nipples were small and dark.

"Touch me," he directed her.

Freed from every inhibition she'd ever had, she did touch him. First she laid her hands lightly against his rib cage. Then she leaned in and tongued one of his nipples.

He groaned in obvious pleasure.

Emboldened, she blazed a trail of kisses up his firm arm to his collarbone. At this point she didn't kid herself, he was in complete control of the situation—standing stoically with his hands lightly resting on her shoulders, enduring her gentle ministrations with scarcely a sign of reaction except the quickness of his breathing.

When her mouth reached his chin, he came to life. His grip on her shoulders tightened. He tilted his head down and angled his mouth over hers, taking possession with one long, slow, wet kiss.

The kiss was a little familiar. She found she didn't even have to summon the memory of how he tasted—it was just there. It was also different, new, more exciting, more frightening, maybe because she knew it wouldn't end there. She slid her hands around his middle and planted them firmly on his back, holding him tightly to her as he thoroughly explored her mouth with little nips and nibbles, then a bold thrust of his tongue.

Tess had never felt anything so wonderful. Closeness was foreign to her, always associated with discomfort, yet there she was practically inside Nate's skin, and she'd never felt better. She'd never felt quite so much a woman, either. Her blood thrummed through her veins, her heart beat wildly, her juices flowed, and the core of her burned with a fire that would not be quenched by anything but total satisfaction.

It kept getting better. Still kissing her with exquisite

thoroughness, Nate moved one hand to her breast. At first he simply held it, letting her get accustomed to the new intimacy. Then he began a slow caress, exploring every square inch before finally focusing on her nipple.

Such sweet torture! Following unfamiliar instincts, she pushed her hips against his, finding the evidence of his arousal pressed against her belly. She reveled in the feel of it, exalted in her sense of feminine power.

"Am I there? Am I with you?"

Nate's voice floated to her from somewhere else. It took her a few disconcerting moments to realize it was the real live Nate, speaking softly into her ear. He had no way of knowing whether he had breached the barriers of her mind unless she told him so.

"Yes, I'm reading you loud and clear," she said a little desperately. "For God's sake, don't stop now!"

"No, no," he murmured soothingly. "I won't."

She was briefly aware of his arms, wrapping themselves more securely around her in the real world; their bodies, though still fully clothed, touching intimately.

Then she was back, fully involved in the fantasy, naked and surrounded by silk and satin.

Nate ended the kiss, then abruptly scooped her up into his arms as if she weighed no more than a cloud. And, she thought dimly, maybe she didn't. This was fantasy, after all.

He eased her down onto the mound of pillows. "I'm going to love you like no woman's ever been loved," he said, as clearly as if they'd been talking in the conscious world. "I'm going to worship every part of your body, from your little toes to your eyebrows, and then I'm going to take you and make you mine—forever mine."

She thrilled to his words even as she acknowledged that she might be embellishing the fantasy. *Forever mine?* Nate wouldn't have said that. They'd never even talked about next week, much less eternity.

But she couldn't devote any more time to analyzing words. He was making good on his promises, kissing her feet, sucking on her toes, finding little hollows and dents and bumps that were incredibly sensitive—places she'd never dreamed could be so erogenous. Writhing with pleasure, she wondered distractedly if she wouldn't be expected to do the same thing to him in reverse. She found herself thinking about touching him intimately, and her whole body flushed and tingled.

He worked his way up, eliciting sighs and giggles and moans of pure pleasure, though he meticulously avoided her most intimate areas. By the time he'd reached the halfway point, she'd reached the end of her patience.

"I'm ready now," she said.

He kissed each of her breasts without comment, lavishing attention on them.

"I'm ready *now*."

He ignored the pleading tone in her voice, taking his time. Surely midnight would come and go by the time he finished reducing her to an abject puddle of wanton desire, but she couldn't change a thing. She was helpless. Deliriously aroused, but helpless.

He did, indeed, finish with her eyebrows. Then he

looked deeply into her eyes. He didn't have to say anything further. She separated her legs, inviting him to become a part of her.

He knelt between her bent knees, then covered her body with his. He gave her a light kiss, almost an apology, and then he slid inside.

Her whole body felt electrified. As Nate thrust inside her the affected nerve endings practically cried out from the stimulation.

Her brain was about to be overloaded with pleasure.

It occurred to her to wonder—if this was his fantasy, how come *she* felt so great?

An exquisite pressure built inside her, demanding release. Was this what she'd heard about and thought would never happen to her? How could those mechanical descriptions she'd read about in sex-education classes translate into this heavenly experience? Or was *her* imagination working overtime? She'd certainly read enough romance novels, with their heavily sensual, overembellished love scenes.

She couldn't devote much attention to wondering about that. She was swamped with sensations. She wanted to laugh and cry at the same time. Then suddenly the earth tilted, and she thought she got a real glimpse of heaven. She cried out from the sheer physical joy of it, of finding such unexpected ecstasy.

Her eyes were closed, both in fantasy and in reality. When she opened them tentatively, she saw not the satin room with its pink-and-lilac pillows, but Nate's dimly lit living room. Her cries seemed to echo around the room, and her throat felt a little raw.

Nate still held on tightly, his face buried against her neck. He spoke first. "You okay?"

"Yes, I think so." She was still trying to figure out what had happened. Though she was definitely back in the here and now, some vestiges of the fantasy remained. The way her body felt, for example. Satiated. Completely and thoroughly satisfied.

"I feel like an idiot asking this, but, did it work?"

She nodded. "Really well." She twisted around so she could see him, then cupped his face with her hand while he looked at her quizzically. "It was the most beautiful . . ." Words failed her. She was surprised to feel tears threatening. "What have I been missing?"

"I wish I'd been there."

"You were!" she insisted.

He shook his head sadly. "It was just a fantasy for me—an especially good one, but completely imaginary—nothing approaching cosmic."

"For an imaginary guy, you sure know how to give a girl a good time."

He grinned, as she'd hoped her bit of male ego stroking would make him do. "You did seem to enjoy yourself."

"How do you know?" she asked suspiciously.

"It was hard to miss."

"Did I . . ."

"That's what it looked like to me."

Tess was torn between being fascinated and embarrassed by her body's behavior. This was all so new to her.

Nate glanced at his watch, suddenly grim again. "We probably should get going. No telling what kinds of roadblocks the Cat has in store to slow us down."

Tess gasped. "Midnight. Midnight—how close are we?" She twisted his arm around to look at the watch. "Nine forty-five?" The entire fantasy had lasted less than ten minutes. It had seemed like hours to her, though she'd heard that earthly time had no meaning in other dimensions.

Surely that's where she'd been—in another dimension.

Reluctantly she slid off Nate's lap. "We'd better get going." Her time with Nate had been a pleasant interlude, but the real world was intruding. "Can you help me take stuff down to the car?"

He stood and touched her arm, stilling her. She looked back at him over her shoulder.

He stroked her cheek. She hoped he would say something about making love for real at a later date. But whatever he was thinking, he kept it to himself. "Sure, I'll help with whatever you need."

Tess had all of her canvas bags stashed neatly by the door with all of the necessary ingredients. All but one. As she and Nate shrugged into jackets, preparing to leave the apartment, she approached him shyly, nail scissors in hand. If she didn't get this done quickly, she would lose her nerve.

"Is that everything?"

"Almost." She reached up with the scissors and snipped off a lock of his hair, then tucked it into a plastic bag. "That's it."

He stared after her, speechless, as she preceded him out the door.

ELEVEN

It took Nate a few moments to recover from the hair snipping. What was the significance? he thought as he followed Tess down the back stairs, watching every step so he wouldn't end up like the shopkeeper, Anne-Louise. What, exactly, did the damn spell say?

The blood of a virgin, and a lock of hair from her own true love.

Holy hell. Did that mean what he thought it meant? Whoa, whoa, he was getting ahead of himself. It didn't mean she was in love with him, just that he was the closest thing to a "true love" she could find. They couldn't very well perform the spell with no one's hair. His would have to do.

He was sure that was all there was to it. Now, though, he couldn't decide whether that conclusion relieved or disappointed him. He'd already acknowledged that his feelings for Tess were more than casual. That something important was happening. But as for a future together . . . how could he deal with the one-sidedness of their relationship? How could he cope with a woman who knew, or could find out, every intimate detail of his life just by touching him, while she remained such a mystery to him?

He couldn't see how it would work.

He and Tess put everything they would need in the backseat of his car, along with the Book of Shadows in case they wanted to refer to something, though Tess had the spell memorized backward and forward. They hadn't driven the car since their flight from Judy's town house two days earlier, because the Cat statue was in the trunk. Now, Nate's trusty Fairlane seemed to groan in protest when he opened the door. Even the car's appearance had taken on sinister qualities.

"Man, I'm losing it," he grumbled, rubbing at the healing scratches Whiskers had given his arm. He supposed he was lucky he didn't have gangrene.

"What?" Tess asked.

"Nothing. Just a minor delusion that my car has turned evil."

"Wouldn't surprise me at this point. Are we ready?" she asked too brightly.

"Ready as we'll ever be."

Their first hurdle came when Nate tried to start his car. Nothing. "I just replaced the battery six months ago," he said on a sigh.

"Maybe we left the lights on last time we were in it," Tess suggested. "We were pretty unnerved."

"Since when did you start trying to assign logical explanations to everything that happens to us?" he groused as he got out of the car. "Let's just chalk another one up to the curse and be done with it. Should we jump the engine, or move everything over to your car?"

"My car," Tess said decisively.

Ten minutes later they were on the road in Tess's Tercel. Right before they'd left, Nate had gingerly transferred the Crimson Cat to Tess's trunk. Was it his imagination, or had the thing been vibrating in his hands? And just before the trunk lid had slammed, he thought he'd seen something glowing in the darkness.

The trip to Sudbury was surprisingly uneventful—no accidents, no falling trees. But a storm was brewing. By the time they turned off the main highway, the winds had picked up considerably, buffeting the car with alarmingly violent gusts. The full moon, now high in the sky, played peekaboo with churning storm clouds.

"Someone's following us," Tess said. "That same car has been behind us ever since we exited the main road."

A few days before, Nate would have thought Tess was being paranoid. But not now. They had to watch anything out of the ordinary carefully. And the car that Tess had pointed out was following a little too close.

Nate slowed down and pulled to the shoulder to let the car pass. At first, the other driver didn't take the hint. But finally the car pulled around and ahead of Nate and Tess.

Tess sighed audibly. "Guess I'm a little skittish."

"Me too."

As they moved into a residential area another car turned from a side street and started to follow. "Ah, hell."

"What?"

"We've got company again, and it's the same car. Want me to try to lose him?"

Tess looked at her watch. "We don't have much time to spare, and I'm not sure my car has enough horses under the hood to lose anyone. Let's just go."

The strange car stayed on their tail all the way to the turnoff for the church and cemetery, but at that point he went on straight.

"Thank God for that," Tess said.

Nate reserved his gratitude. He'd tailed people a time or two. Sometimes he would deliberately *not* turn, just to throw off his prey, then double back or catch them at another intersection.

They were still blessedly alone, however, when they pulled into the church parking lot. The wind was blowing hard, whistling eerily through the wrought-iron fence that protected the graveyard. The huge hardwood trees that surrounded them groaned in protest.

Nate took one look through the fence at the gravestones within and felt his skin go clammy. The way the moonlight wavered and flickered made the stone markers move, as if they were dancing. Visions of every B horror movie he'd ever seen danced through his mind. Carrie's hand pushing through the dirt of her new grave. Zombies lurching around with their empty eyes and green skin.

"Nate? Nate!"

"Huh? Oh, sorry. I zoned out there for a minute." He'd been standing frozen beside the car. "Let's carry this stuff to the fence. Then you can climb over and I'll hand everything to you."

"Okay. I hope it doesn't rain." At her words, the first fat drops began falling. "Well, so much for that."

When it came to carrying the cat, Tess insisted it was her turn. Up until now, she hadn't actually come into physical contact with the statue. She leaned inside the trunk and picked it up, still wrapped in its paper bag.

She hadn't gone more than a few steps toward the fence when she cried out and dropped the statue into the grass.

"What's wrong?" Nate demanded, at her side in an instant.

"It burned me!" She held out her hands. Even in the on-again, off-again moonlight, Nate could see the angry red welts on the palms of her hands.

"Holy—! Are you okay? Do you need medical—"

"No, it's not that bad. Hurts like hell. I've got some old towels in the trunk I use at the car wash. Maybe we can use them like pot holders—"

"That won't be necessary."

Nate and Tess froze, looking around for the source of the voice that didn't belong to either of them. Nate recognized it, though.

A shadow stepped from behind a massive tree trunk. Tristan Solca stood before them, and this time he didn't wait before displaying his knife, an even bigger knife than he'd used before. It glittered malevolently in the moonlight, as did his black eyes. "All I want is the statue. That's simple enough, isn't it?"

All of Tess's oxygen seemed to be trapped in her throat. They couldn't get this close, only to be thwarted by this horrible man who wanted to use the Cat for who knew what evil purposes.

Well, he'd have to take it over her dead body.

"Look, Solca, give us half an hour," Nate said, using his best cajoling voice. "We're about to use the statue for a small . . . exercise. A religious ceremony, if you will. After we're done, you can have the Cat. And we won't even press charges for assault with a deadly weapon, which this in fact is. Fair enough?"

Solca's face wavered with uncertainty.

"That okay with you, Tess?" Nate looked over at her.

She nodded, though she didn't have a good feeling about this. What if the spell failed? How could they, in good conscience, hand over an instrument of evil power to this horrible man?

"What kind of ceremony?" Solca asked suspiciously.

"Just a little witchly hocus-pocus," Nate said glibly. It was the wrong thing to say.

Solca's eyes narrowed dangerously. "You're going to take the curse off it!" He turned his head and spat. "Morganna attempted and failed. It can't be done."

"Then why don't you let us get on with it?" Tess

said. "We'll try, we'll fail, we'll probably die in the process, and you can have your old Cat."

Solca wavered again. "Why should I take the chance? Morganna always said her spawn had powers she only dreamed of. You might succeed at that." He took a step forward.

Tess and Nate instinctively moved closer together, protecting the hated Crimson Cat between them. "I wouldn't recommend it," Nate said.

"You think those fancy kung-fu steps of yours are any match for a man with a knife?" Solca challenged. His teeth glowed yellow in the moonlight. He took another step, his eyes on Nate.

Nate adopted a fighting stance.

Oh, God, Tess thought, she couldn't let Nate get hurt. She was just about to speak up and tell Solca he could have his damn statue when all at once the man lunged at *her*.

The move was so completely unexpected, it knocked both Tess and Nate off balance. Before she knew what was happening, the knife sliced downward faster than she could see, and her left arm was cut—deep.

Nate's attention immediately went to Tess, no doubt as Solca had anticipated. He made a grab for the Cat and started running with it.

"Go after him!" Tess cried, barely able to get the words out through the pain in her arm. She clamped her other hand over the cut and hugged her arm against her, trying to stanch the flow of blood. "I'm okay. Don't let him leave with the Cat."

After a moment of indecision Nate took off after Solca. He was both bigger and faster than the other man, and it took him only a few seconds to overtake the Gypsy and tackle him, like an all-pro linebacker. Solca fumbled the statue. It went flying while the two men hit the ground.

"Nate!" Tess ran to where the two men grappled with each other. Solca still had the knife, but Nate had a firm grip around the man's wrist. The blade was inches from Nate's neck.

Tess dropped to her knees, grabbed Solca's arm, and bit him. He screamed and dropped the knife, which she promptly recovered and flung out into the darkness where it couldn't hurt anyone.

Without his weapon, Solca was helpless. He stopped struggling and, to Tess's horror, began sobbing. "My Cat . . . my Cat."

Nate stood up and brushed himself off. The other man lay on the ground curled into the fetal position. "What should we do with him now?"

"We could tie him up, or lock him in the trunk of the car," Tess suggested. "Just until we finish the spell. Whatever we do, we have to hurry. Midnight's coming fast."

"The trunk will have to do, I guess." Nate dragged Solca onto his feet.

All at once the little man came alive. He gave Nate a vicious punch in the gut, shook himself free, and took off into the darkness.

"Nate! Nate, are you all right?"

"I'm not . . . worried . . . about me," he said,

trying to straighten up. "I'm . . . worried about . . . you. You're bleeding like a . . ." He couldn't finish. He leaned against a tree, trying to catch his breath.

"I was going to have to cut myself anyway," Tess said. "Solca just saved me the trouble. Let's just do the spell before he works up his nerve and comes back with something worse than a knife."

Nate nodded. "You're sure you aren't bleeding to death?"

"The bleeding is slowing down," she fibbed. If she didn't, he would run her straight to a hospital.

Something caught her eye. It was the Crimson Cat peeking at her from the grass where it had fallen, its golden gemstone eyes glowing with a light all their own.

"I'll get it." Nate had seen the eyes too. He took off his belt, hooked it around the Cat's neck. Then he looked up at her. "Jeez, Tess, the blood . . ." He looked a little pale himself.

"I'm okay, really. Just go, hurry. We don't have much time."

Looking doubtful, Nate shrugged and dragged the statue across the ground toward the cemetery.

Tess followed, feeling a little light-headed—whether from the fright she'd just had, or the loss of blood, she didn't know. There was a lot of blood on the front of her sweater, but it was hard for her to judge how much she'd really lost. The arm was still bleeding, though. She could feel the warmth seeping between her fingers as she applied pressure with her other hand.

With Nate's help, Tess managed to clamber over the wrought-iron gate. He handed her the tools and ingredients for the spell. When it came time to transfer the Cat, he unceremoniously heaved it over the fence. It landed with a thunk on the soft ground.

"I can't believe I ever thought that thing was striking," he grumbled as he vaulted over the fence himself, apparently recovered from Solca's sucker punch.

Abruptly Nate froze, and Tess remembered his aversion to cemeteries. "Nate?"

"Mmm?" He was breathing hard, as if he'd just run a couple of miles.

"You don't have to do this, you know. I can cast the spell by myself."

"Now, what kind of wuss would I be if I let you do that, hmm?" He grabbed up three of the bags, leaving the fourth for her, and started gamely toward the interior of the cemetery. "Which way?"

Tess picked up the remaining bag and set out after him, her heart swelling. How could she not love a man who would face his demons for her? Oh, Lord, she did love him. A surge of confidence coursed through her veins. The spell was going to work. It had to.

Nate tried to block out the sights around him and focus solely on his objective, which was to reach the grave of the poor, ill-fated girl Tess had chosen without losing his dinner. *There's nothing here that can hurt you,* he told himself over and over. But phobias did not respond well to logic, he discovered. Besides, there was something there that could hurt him. The Crimson Cat thump-thumped along at his heel. He half expected it to take a bite out of his ankle.

Tess wandered around a bit until she found the grave marker with the bow on top. "There it is!" she shouted triumphantly when she spotted it. She picked up her step, holding her canvas bags with one hand, her injured arm clutched against her chest.

The sight of all that blood scared him more than the leering gravestones did. Was she really all right? He'd considered bundling her up and heading for a hospital, but he knew that if he did, she would never forgive him for messing up their one and only chance to cast the spell. He could have argued that they always had next month, but by then it might be too late for Judy, and possibly too late for them.

That fear overrode everything else. He couldn't escape the certainty that if they didn't get this spell-casting thing right the first time, nothing would ever be right again.

"Stand here," Tess directed. Instantly there was an otherworldliness about her that he hadn't seen before, an air of supernatural authority, as if she'd suddenly found her element. He stood where she indicated, at the foot of the grave, and stared in awe as he realized he really was in love with a witch.

"I'm going to cast a circle of protection," she said. "No matter what happens, don't step outside of it." Then she set some incense alight in her little censer and stood it atop the gravestone, where it gently smoked. She poured some water in her cup, added a few pinches of various powders, then dipped her athame into the concoction and walked a wide circle around him and the grave, the knife pointed to the ground.

She spoke some ritual words, but with the wind blowing and the quietness of her voice, he caught only a few words now and again. She seemed to be asking for help from archangels.

He'd read *nothing* about archangels in that Book of Shadows, so he could only assume that she was drawing on long-suppressed memories of Morganna's teachings—or maybe it was just raw instinct. The sight of her working so purposefully, her face infused with serious intent, made him shiver. He felt the faint stirrings of desire for her rearing its ugly head, so he ruthlessly suppressed them. It didn't seem appropriate to bring sexual desire into this high—almost sacred—ritual.

Whatever his personal feelings for her, at that moment he believed in magic with all his heart and soul, and he felt her power. If anyone could pull off this spell, it was Tess.

When she completed the circle of protection, Nate's ears began to ring. From the corner of his eye, the circle she'd drawn seemed to glow with a faint blue fire, though when he looked at it directly, the flames disappeared.

Next, Tess wiped out the cup with a white cloth. She poured wine into the chalice, then stepped over to Nate, her eyes overly bright. "Drink."

"Is this part of the spell?" he asked, positive he hadn't read anything about *drinking* the wine.

"No. I just figured you could use a slug. I know I could." He obliged by taking a sip of the cheap wine, and she did the same. It brought a little color to her overly pale face. "Besides, drinking from the same cup should bind our energies. I think."

She stepped away and returned to the tedium of the ritual of adding various ingredients to the cup of wine. When she crushed the ash leaves in her hand and dropped them into the brew, thunder rumbled menacingly around them, and the wind whistling through the surrounding tombstones sounded like the wailing of a hundred lost souls. The patter of rain, in earnest this time, fell all around them.

"Now be gone this hex," she said, her voice loud and clear. Then she slowly poured the wine mixture onto the ground at her feet. "May the innocence of this lost one, the purity of her soul, threefold reverse the evil power embodied by the Crimson Cat."

Lightning flashed, and thunder cracked again, louder this time. Nate rubbed at his eyes. When he opened them again, he looked down at the statue, which he'd abandoned a couple of feet from where he stood. The gold eyes were definitely glowing.

Then it moved.

The tail switched, the teeth were bared, the ears flattened against its head.

"No!" The strangled denial came from deep in his throat.

Tess focused her otherworldly gaze on him, obviously alarmed.

He had to fight the urge to grab Tess and run for the fence, for surely his sanity could be regained on the outside. "It's moving," he said, pointing down at the statue. But when he looked at it again, it was once more inanimate red stone.

"It's playing with your mind," Tess said, raising her voice against the ever-louder roar of the wind. "Don't leave the circle!"

He nodded, wanting to close his eyes, but he couldn't tear his gaze away from Tess, his beautiful, wondrous Tess as she continued with the ritual.

She seemed to be getting weaker—or was that his imagination too? Was that deathly pallor a trick of the moonlight, or was her injury more severe than she'd led him to believe? The bloodstain on the front of her shirt had definitely grown.

Suddenly she dropped the chalice, staring at him with alarm. "Nate!"

"What?"

Then she shook her head and looked at him again. "There was something behind you, like a demon . . . but it's gone now."

"It's not real. Finish the spell. It's about one minute till midnight."

"Bring me the Cat," she said, new steel in her voice.

He dragged the statue to the place she indicated, then removed the belt. Her voice battled the wind again:

> *"By the virgin's lifeblood and the purity of her*
>   *love,*
> *and by the power of the words here spoken,*
> *the four elements of the universe unite under*
> *the goddess moon, the evil spell be broken!"*

With that she extended her arm toward the Crimson Cat. Her blood flowed freely from the cut, and for the first time Nate got a good look at how deeply she'd been wounded.

"Tess, my God!"

Her blood dripped onto the statue. Each drop sizzled when it made contact, as if it had hit a hot griddle. In Tess's other hand was the lock she'd snipped from Nate's head. She held it aloft, opened her hand, and let the wind scatter the hair to the four corners.

"Almost done," she said. "One more thing." She bent down and tried to pick up the statue, but her strength was spent.

Nate picked it up for her. It was warm to the touch, but it didn't burn him, as if perhaps its power was already waning. "What do you want me to do with it?"

"Hold it up to the sky." She placed her hands on the statue also, and they stood with it overhead, chest to chest. The smell of electricity filled the air, and her hair stood on end as she spoke one last time. "May the power of this curse be channeled to good, may the evil be undone, an' it harm none, so mote it be!"

The final word of the spell had barely cleared her lips when an earsplitting crack rent the air. A bolt of lightning struck the statue. Nate felt the charge go through his arms, his body, and out his feet. He staggered, dropped, and the world went black.

When he awoke, it was to a gentle rain falling. A clock somewhere nearby was chiming midnight, so he couldn't have been out for long. He shook his head, trying to regain his senses. Had he just survived a direct hit by lightning?

Then he saw Tess. She lay crumpled on the ground, pale, unmoving. By her side was a pile of red dust—all that was left of the Crimson Cat.

TWELVE

Nate said a few words that should not have been uttered on consecrated ground. What the hell were they doing fooling around in a graveyard when Tess was bleeding? He scooped her up and, leaving everything else behind, ran toward the fence. Later he wasn't sure how he did it, but he kicked the gate open, breaking the lock.

"Please be all right, Tess." He deposited her gently into the passenger seat of her car, then took the extra time to fasten the shoulder harness around her. Her blood was everywhere—on her, on him. He'd never been so scared in his life.

Lurking in a corner of the parking lot, Nate thought he saw the shadow of a man—Tristan Solca. But the pathetic creature was too timid now even to approach. Nate felt a pang of pity for the poor man, forever stripped of the power he'd come to depend on, to hope for.

Nate jumped in the car, started it up, then couldn't decide where to go. A local hospital? He didn't even know where one was. Rather than waste time asking someone, he decided to drive straight to Mass General. At this hour of the night he could make it in twenty minutes.

He kept up a monologue through the next few minutes, a pep talk aimed at Tess but intended for himself. "You can't die on me, Tess," he admonished. "Not when I just figured out I love you. We're bonded, remember? We drank the wine. I made love to you in your mind. Not many guys can claim that, I bet."

She was frighteningly still and quiet.

"C'mon, Tess, just hold on. Another few minutes and you'll have the finest medical care in the country." He thought he heard her sigh. Was that good or bad? It meant she was breathing, at least.

"N-Nate?"

Yes! "I'm here, sweetheart. You're hurt. I'm taking you to the hospital. Can you hold on for me?"

"Yes. For you."

Gradually Tess's senses returned. She knew she was in her car, and that Nate was driving incredibly fast. Then she remembered. "The spell?"

"Yeah."

"Did we finish?"

"I think so. The same lightning bolt that knocked us down for the count turned the Crimson Cat into a pile of sand. I'd say that was a definite sign you did something right."

That sounded promising. But they wouldn't know for sure that they'd succeeded until they found out about Judy.

"I'm tired," Tess said, her eyes drooping.

"I'm not surprised. Curse busting is exhausting work, and draining a couple of quarts of your own blood probably didn't do much for your energy level."

She closed her eyes, secure in the knowledge that Nate would take care of her.

When she woke a little later, she was in a hospital treatment room with a medical team bustling around her. Needles stabbed her arms and a mask covered her face.

"There she is," a doctor-looking person said, peering at her from over his own mask. "It's okay, Tess, you're going to be fine. Just relax." As he said this he flashed a small penlight in first one eye, then the other.

"Nate?"

"He's in the waiting room," a nurse piped up. "He's fine too. We'll let you see him as soon as we get a little more blood pumped into you."

Tess winced as another needle pierced her arm.

"That's just the anesthetic, honey. We're getting ready to stitch you up."

She decided she'd just as soon sleep through this part, but she remained maddeningly alert, more so by the minute. The frenzy around her had settled down now that she'd shown the medical team she wasn't going to die on them.

"Judy!" she said suddenly. "Has anyone checked on her? Judy Cosgrove. She's in ICU."

The doctor and nurse working on Tess looked at each other and shrugged. The nurse addressed Tess. "Let's get you fixed up first. Then we'll check on Julie."

"Judy, not Julie!" With her free hand, though it had a lot of tubes connected to it, Tess pulled off her oxygen mask. "Get Nate in here right now. I mean it. Now, or I'm refusing any further treatment."

"Sheesh," the nurse muttered, "she gets a little blood in her and she gets all uppity. Serena," she called to one of the other nurses who was just peeling off her rubber gloves, "go get her guy and bring him back here." The nurse put a firm hand on Tess's shoulder. "You lie still and let the doctor stitch."

Nate appeared mere seconds later. He looked like holy hell, all covered with blood—her blood, she realized—but he was a welcome sight all the same. He was walking and talking—and smiling, just for her.

"Nate."

"Look at you," he said, stroking her cheek. "Back with the living. Don't ever scare me like that again."

His touch was warm and reassuring and . . . something else. She pressed her face against his palm. "Nate, think of something."

"What?"

"Anything. Think of a number from one to ten."

"Uh, okay."

She closed her eyes. "Seven?"

"Three."

They looked at each other, eyes wide. "I can't read your mind! Look, look," Tess said, gesturing toward the medical people working on her stitches, "these people are touching the hell out of me, and I'm not getting anything—no vibrations, no thought forms, nothing. Maybe that bolt of lightning rearranged my electrons or something."

The doctor and nurse glanced over at her briefly, then returned to their task. She supposed they'd heard more bizarre utterings in the ER.

"Is this a good thing?" Nate asked cautiously.

"Well, yeah. I mean, I never wanted to be psychic in the first place. Now apparently I'm not." But it was kind of weird. She'd taken her gift for granted for so long, she never realized what it would feel like if it were suddenly gone.

"You don't look happy."

"Oh, never mind about that," she said abruptly. "What about Judy?"

"I tried to check on her, but since I wasn't family, they wouldn't give me any information."

That didn't bode well, Tess thought, deflating. The hospital had never denied either of them information before. "Let's go up to her room and check." She turned to the doctor. "Are you about done with those stitches?"

The nurse scowled. "You aren't going anywhere, missy. You came in here half-dead from loss of blood, and we pulled off at least half a miracle bringing you back. You're going to lie here quietly until we get you a room. Sheesh!"

The doctor scowled at her too. "What she said."

Tess slumped back onto the gurney. The pain in her arm was nothing compared with the pain of not knowing Judy's condition. What if the spell had failed? What if Judy died? Would they wait until the next full moon and try again, or give it up and submit to the curse?

That was a dismal thought. She supposed she ought to be grateful she and Nate had at least survived the ordeal. The same couldn't be said about the Crimson Cat.

The doctor and nurse finished with Tess's arm and quietly withdrew, leaving her alone with Nate. He grabbed the rolling stool abandoned by the doctor and sat down, then rubbed her upper arm lightly—the only part of her arm that didn't have needles sticking out of it.

"You look pretty good, considering," he said. "At least you've got some color back in your cheeks. How do you feel?"

"Not bad."

"How are your hands?"

"Those IV needles are murder."

"No, I mean the burns."

She looked at him. "Burns?" She turned her hand over and slowly opened her curled fingers. The palm of her right hand was pink and healthy.

"You had second-degree burns on that hand a couple of hours ago," Nate said excitedly. "From picking up the cat, remember?"

She did remember! "Well, my hands are fine now.

Oh, Nate, do you think—does that mean we did it? We reversed the curse?"

He grinned ear to ear. "I think maybe we did." Then his grin faded. "But did we do it in time for Judy?"

An orderly entered the treatment room. "I'm supposed to take you to your room. Two-oh-three."

"Okay," Tess said meekly. Then she whispered to Nate, "Second floor. Same as ICU."

When the orderly rolled her gurney off the elevator on the second floor, Tess spoke up again. "Go left."

"Pardon me?"

"Turn me to the left and down that hall. Toward ICU."

"But your room—"

"I want to take the scenic route, okay?"

He shrugged and did as she asked. When they approached the ICU doors, they immediately saw that a great commotion was taking place inside. Nurses running around like determined ants. When someone came barreling out the ICU doors, loud voices drifted out into the hallway.

"Oh, no," Tess breathed. "What if we were too late? Take me inside," she told the orderly. "Hurry."

"What do you think this is, a taxi service?"

"Please. My friend is in there. I just want to see if she's okay."

The orderly clearly thought she was a candidate for the psych ward, but he pushed her gurney through the double doors. "You can do the explaining when we get stopped."

Then she heard it. Judy's voice, high and clear and strong. "Coma? I was in a coma? No way. You guys are exaggerating."

Tess looked at Nate. His grin matched hers.

"We did it!" they said together.

The orderly merely shook his head. "Enough of this. My orders say room two-oh-three, and that's where you're going."

Tess came home from the hospital two days later, feeling remarkably fit. Nate had stayed with her almost the entire time. When she was released, he'd insisted on driving her home, getting her settled, fixing her a grilled-cheese sandwich and tomato soup.

Tess figured that pretty soon he'd run out of things to do for her. She wondered how she could keep him around. One thought did occur to her. After he'd made love to her in his mind, she'd decided she was going to make it happen for real—as soon as possible.

Now would be a good time. But what if he didn't see things her way? They'd been in the throes of a very emotional situation. Now that things were getting back to normal, maybe he felt differently about her. She had no idea how to broach the subject. He'd been unfailingly kind since her recovery in the ER, but nothing sexual had passed between them, not even a wink.

After cleaning up the lunch dishes, he came into the living room and sat down next to her on the couch, where she reclined in her peach silk robe like some invalid only because he'd ordered her to rest.

"I'll be going back to the office in a couple of days," she said, feeling awkward. "I'll bet my work has piled up like crazy."

"Yeah, I need to go back to work pretty soon too."

"To write up the Moonbeam Majick story?" she asked. "I won't try to stop you. The story is as much yours as mine now."

He laughed. "Tess. Get real. Who would believe it? No, I'm going back to that antiques story I was working on."

"You mean that was a real story? Not just a ruse to get to me?"

"It started out as a ruse, but it turned into something pretty intriguing. *Boston Life* magazine is interested in it."

They fell silent. She looked around the room desperately, trying to find inspiration. If she didn't say something, he was going to leave! But her living room was so damn white, so damn devoid of anything that might make a topic of conversation. How had she ever thought it was comforting?

"I'm going to buy some more colorful paintings for the walls," she declared. "Abstracts. And maybe an Oriental rug."

"Your decor is a little on the minimal side."

"Nothing like your apartment," she said wistfully. "I really like your place. It's so homey, so comfortable."

"So, move in with me."

Now the silence crackled with electricity.

"Maybe I will," she finally said, peering covertly at him through her lashes to gauge his reaction.

He smiled and gently pulled her against him, then lay back with her in his arms. "We could find a bigger place, if you want."

She closed her eyes, picturing it. It would look something like Nate's place, but less crowded. She liked her white sofas, but some colorful throws would make them better. They could have a real library, for all of Nate's books and magazines.

And definitely a bigger kitchen.

"You'd like a bigger kitchen, wouldn't you?" he asked.

Oh. He'd read her mind again. "Mm, yes." Were they still psychically linked? Even though her gift, as far as she could tell, had vanished? She relaxed and opened her mind to the possibilities.

Hell, how am I ever going to get her to marry me? She heard his voice as clearly as if he were speaking aloud, but she knew he wasn't. *We've known each other, what, a week? How is it possible for anyone to know they want to spend the rest of their lives together after only a week?*

She knew she should stop him, tell him that she was tuned into his frequency, but she couldn't get any words past the lump in her throat.

Still, there is that lock-of-hair thing. The spell worked, didn't it? That must mean she loves me.

"Yes, of course I love you," Tess said through tears of joy.

Nate jumped. "I thought you—"

"I thought I did, too, but apparently I didn't lose

everything. I can still read at least some of your thoughts. Do you mind having a wife who can tune into you like that?" She twisted around to look at him.

A slow, lazy smile spread across his face. "Since I'd never cheat on you, or lie to you, I guess it doesn't bother me that much. Like you once said, I'll get used to it."

"Good. In that case, yes, I'll marry you."

"I haven't asked, yet."

"But you want to. Maybe you should do it after we make love." She maneuvered herself onto her stomach so she was lying on top of him in a very intimate position. She let her robe fall open just a little, and was rewarded by a flash of desire in his eyes.

"Tess," he objected, "you're still recovering. I wouldn't even think of—"

"Please, think of it," she said. And she planted a slow, wet kiss on his surprised mouth. "Virginity is tedious at my age. Let's put an end to it. I'm feeling fine, really."

Nate hesitated only a fraction of a second longer before he kissed her back. "If you're sure . . ."

"Yes."

They ended up on the floor, surrounded by her pastel silk pillows. The scene was very reminiscent of the fantasy in some ways, though different in others. For one thing, Nate's clothes didn't magically vanish. She had to tug to get them all off, and she laughed until her stomach hurt when, in their frenzy, he got his foot stuck in the leg of his jeans.

When he was finally naked, though, all laughter

stopped. He was a beautiful specimen of the male species. Whereas her fantasy had featured everything in soft focus, now all was sharply defined—sights, sounds, even smells. She hadn't realized how delicious Nate's skin smelled, or how the texture of his hair felt against her face.

Nate was infinitely patient, caressing and kissing her everywhere until she begged him to put an end to her misery. She gasped when he touched her between her legs, and nearly dissolved when he slipped his finger insider her. No fantasy could have done this experience justice.

"You are a hot woman, Tess DeWitt," he whispered. "But I'm still afraid I'll hurt you."

That seemed impossible. Nothing could hurt her, not while Nate Wagner was loving her. Between them, their love was more powerful than a centuries-old curse. "We're already one in mind and soul," she said. "It's time for us to be one in body."

Nate groaned and kissed her again. "You said that really well."

He nudged her legs apart and moved between them. Tess wondered how a man his size could manage to lie so gently atop her, but he felt no heavier than a pillow. She rejoiced when his hardness sought entrance to her body. She exulted when he plunged inside.

Unlike their shared fantasy, she felt momentary pain. It surprised her enough that a few little tears sprang into her eyes. Nate, attuned to her as he was, immediately stilled.

"I did hurt you."

"It was inevitable," she said, laughing. "It's not as bad as all that." She laughed again. "It's gone now. Please don't stop." She closed her eyes and bit her lip and new, more pleasurable sensations made themselves known. "It feels wonderful now."

He began moving again, slowly, letting her catch up. Then they were flying together, soaring above the stars.

"Tess! I can't . . . wait. . . ."

There was no need for him to prolong his pleasure. She climaxed with a high, keening scream that rattled the furniture. With one final groan he joined her, and she knew that whatever plane she'd been transported to, he'd been there with her.

The oneness was incredible.

"What you do to me," she said when she could talk again.

"Me too."

"Does this mean I can't wear white at the wedding?" she said with a giggle.

"You can wear purple, for all I care," he said, hugging her close just as the phone rang. "Ah, hell, never fails. You're going to let it ring, aren't you?"

"It might be Judy," Tess said, scrambling off the floor. "Just stay right there, I won't be long." She lunged for the extension on the end table. "Hello?"

"Tess? It's Heidi Pavel—from Dowling?"

"Oh, my God, is something wrong with Morganna?" The sanitarium *never* called her.

"No, no, quite the contrary. We've had something of a breakthrough, in fact."

Tess's heart skipped a beat. Was it possible? The spell had cured the burns on her hands and had brought Judy out of her coma, but could it have helped Morganna as well?

"Her doctor doesn't know quite what to make of it, but your mother is asking for you. Would you like to speak to her?"

"Yes!"

There was a long pause, then, incredibly, her mother's voice was on the other end of the line. "Tess? Darling?" She sounded tentative, as if she were afraid Tess would reject her.

"I'm here, Morganna."

"Please, don't call me that. I know I told you to, but couldn't you forget all about that and call me Mother? Just this once?"

Tess's eyes filled with tears. "Yes, Mother, of course."

Mildred DeWitt lowered her voice. "You did it, didn't you? The spell?"

"Yes. Nate and I did it together. The Crimson Cat is gone."

"Then you must have done it correctly—the part I messed up, I mean."

Tess couldn't believe it. She was having a normal conversation with her mother—not Morganna Majick, but the kind mother she remembered from so long ago. "Yes," she managed. "It was love that finally triumphed over evil. True, pure love."

Nate, sensing the importance of the call, had come over to put his arm around Tess. She tipped the receiver out so he could hear both sides of the conversation.

"Love," Mildred repeated. "That's a rare thing in this world. So, when's the wedding?"

Tess, startled, took a few moments to answer. She looked at Nate. He shrugged. "It's, um—"

"Oh, it doesn't matter when," Mildred said. "Just so I'm invited. Your man, your Nate, he must be a good one, though I can't imagine what he must think of me. Can you bring yourself to let me come to the wedding, Tess? I won't embarrass you. Can you possibly ever forgive all those terrible things I did and said?"

Nate nodded his encouragement to Tess.

"Yes, Mother," she said, her heart so full, she thought it would burst with joy. "I can forgive."

She hung up, thinking of all the things she could do now that she never dreamed of—touching, for one thing. The Crimson Cat might have been cursed, but in a way it had turned out to be a blessing in disguise. Without its influence, she might never have gotten her mother back.

And she might never have bonded with Nate, or discovered her own hidden strengths. She might never have known the pure, twenty-four-karat joy of loving and being loved.

"I love you," she said to Nate, at the exact same time he said it to her. They stared at each other, then laughed.

"I'm afraid this marriage won't hold much mystery for either one of us," Nate said, though he didn't seem bothered at all by the idea. "In another week we'll know everything there is to know about each other."

"Then we'll just have to work at being mysterious, huh?" Tess quipped. "Like, I bet right now, you don't know what I'm thinking about doing with some chocolate syrup."

He smiled devilishly. "But I can guess." They raced each other to the fridge.

THE EDITORS' CORNER

The heat is on and nowhere is that more evident than right here at Loveswept. This month's selections include some of our most romantic titles yet. Take one mechanic, one television talk-show host, a masseuse, and a travel agent, then combine them with strong, to-die-for heroes, and you've got yourself one heck of a month's worth of love stories.

Loveswept favorite Mary Kay McComas returns with **ONE ON ONE**, LOVESWEPT #894. Mechanic Michelin Albee has no idea what she's getting into when she picks up stranded motorist Noah Tessler on a lonely stretch of desert highway. Noah's purpose in coming to Gypsum, Nevada, is to meet the woman who captured his late brother's heart and gave birth to Eric, Noah's only living relative. Uncharacteristically, Mich takes a liking to Noah. Trusting him more than she's trusted any man in the past few years, she confides in him about her worries for Eric. As

Noah gets closer to both Mich and her son, will he be able to keep his secret? Once again Mary Kay McComas grabs our hearts in a book as deliciously romantic as a bouquet of wildflowers in a teacup!

In Kathy Lynn Emerson's latest contribution, we learn that love is best when it's **TRIED AND TRUE**, LOVESWEPT #895. Because Vanessa Dare has more than a passing interest in history, she agrees to produce a documentary about professor Grant Bradley's living history center in western New York. Grant knows that having the television talk-show host on the project will bring him the exposure Westbrook Farm needs, but he's surprised when desire sizzles between them. When Nessa doesn't balk at sacrificing present-day comforts, Grant realizes he just might have found the perfect woman. She's content merely to get away from the pressures of work, and as they play the part of an 1890s courting couple, the sweet hunger that transpires could prove to be their destiny. As riveting as the pages of a secret diary, Kathy Lynn Emerson's delectable story of love's mysteries and history's magic is utterly charming.

Donna Kauffman is at her best when she gives us a witty romp, and **TEASE ME**, LOVESWEPT #896, is nothing less. Tucker Morgan knows that his life needs a change. He's just not so sure that posing as a masseur is a change for the better. But since he promised his aunt Lillian he'd investigate the shady goings-on at her Florida retirement community, he'd better take a serious look at those instructional videos she gave him. Sent in to evaluate the new masseur's skills, Lainey Cooper knew she was in trouble from the moment he touched her. If his magical hands turned her knees to mush, Lord knew what he could do to the rest of her body! Aunt Lillian is sure something's happening at Sunset Shores, and insists Lainey and

Tucker team up to uncover its secrets . . . and if a little romance is thrown in on the side, hey, what more can an elderly aunt ask for her nephew? Donna Kauffman delivers a sparkling tale of equal parts mystery and matchmaking.

Welcome Suzanne McMinn, who makes her Loveswept debut with **UNDENIABLE, LOVESWEPT** #897. After his wife left him stranded with four daughters to raise, Garth Holloway decided he wasn't going to add any more women to his life. And when his pretty neighbor Kelly Thompson popped out of a Halloween casket, scaring his youngest child nearly to death, he knew his decision was right. Kelly isn't going to argue with him. She's through with raising children. With her younger siblings now in college, she's free to go wherever her heart desires. But when an undeniable passion reigns, Garth and Kelly can't stay away from each other. His children adore her, not to mention the family dog. Garth doesn't want to hold her back, but faced with unconditional love, will Kelly grab her passport or surrender her solo ticket for a hunk on the family plan? Suzanne McMinn's tale of dreams deferred and temptations tasted is as heartwarming as it is irresistible.

Happy reading!

With warmest wishes,

Susann Brailey   *Joy Abella*

Susann Brailey   Joy Abella
Senior Editor   Administrative Editor

P.S. Look for these women's fiction titles coming in July! Deborah Smith returns with **WHEN VENUS FELL**. A novel of two sisters, seeking refuge from their troubled past, who find love and acceptance amid the shattered remains of a tight-knit family in the mountains of Tennessee. From nationally bestselling author Kay Hooper comes **FINDING LAURA**, now available in paperback. A collector of mirrors, struggling artist Laura Sutherland stumbles across an antique hand mirror that lands her in the midst of the powerful Kilbourne family and a legacy of deadly intent. And fun and laughter abound in **FINDING MR. RIGHT** by Bantam newcomer Emily Carmichael. A femme fatale must return to Earth to find the right man for her best friend. The trouble is, when you're a Welsh corgi, there's only so much you can do to play matchmaker! And immediately following this page, preview the Bantam women's fiction titles on sale in July.

For current information on Bantam's women's fiction, visit our website at the following address:
http://www.bdd.com/romance

Don't miss these exciting
novels from Bantam Books!

On sale in June:

GENUINE LIES
by *Nora Roberts*

THE HOSTAGE BRIDE
by *Jane Feather*

THE WEDDING CHASE
by *Rebecca Kelley*

Genuine Lies
BY NORA ROBERTS

She was a legend. A product of time and talent and her own unrelenting ambition. Eve Benedict. Men thirty years her junior desired her. Women envied her. Studio heads courted her, knowing that in this day when movies were made by accountants, her name was solid gold. In a career that had spanned nearly fifty years, Eve Benedict had known the highs, and the lows, and used both to forge herself into what she wanted to be.

She did as she chose, personally and professionally. If a role interested her, she went after it with the same verve and ferocity she'd used to get her first part. If she desired a man, she snared him, discarding him only when she was done, and—she liked to brag—never with malice. All of her former lovers, and they were legion, remained friends. Or had the good sense to pretend to be.

At sixty-seven, Eve had maintained her magnificent body through discipline and the surgeon's art. Over a half century she had honed herself into a sharp blade. She had used both disappointment and triumph to temper that blade into a weapon that was feared and respected in the kingdom of Hollywood.

She had been a goddess. Now she was a queen with a keen mind and keen tongue. Few knew her heart. None knew her secrets.

◆————◆

Julia wasn't certain if she'd just been given the world's most fascinating Christmas present or an enormous lump of coal. She stood at the big bay window of her Connecticut home and watched the wind hurl the snow in a blinding white dance. Across the room, the logs snapped and sizzled in the wide stone fireplace. A bright red stocking hung on either end of the mantel. Idly, she spun a silver star and sent it twirling on its bough of the blue spruce.

The tree was square in the center of the window, precisely where Brandon had wanted it. They had chosen the six-foot spruce together, had hauled it, puffing and blowing, into the living room, then had spent an entire evening decorating. Brandon had known where he'd wanted every ornament. When she would have tossed the tinsel at the branches in hunks, he had insisted on draping individual strands.

He'd already chosen the spot where they would plant it on New Year's Day, starting a new tradition in their new home in a new year.

At ten, Brandon was a fiend for tradition. Perhaps, she thought, because he had never known a traditional home. Thinking of her son, Julia looked down at the presents stacked under the tree. There, too, was order. Brandon had a ten-year-old's need to shake and sniff and rattle the brightly wrapped boxes. He had the curiosity, and the wit, to cull out hints on what was hidden inside. But when he replaced a box, it went neatly into its space.

In a few hours he would begin to beg his mother to let him open one—just one—present tonight, on Christmas Eve. That, too, was tradition. She would refuse. He would cajole. She would pretend reluctance. He would persuade. And this year, she thought, at last, they would celebrate their Christmas in a real home. Not in an apartment in downtown Manhattan, but a house, a home, with a yard made for snowmen, a big kitchen designed for baking cookies. She'd so badly needed to be able to give him all this. She hoped it helped to make up for not being able to give him a father.

Turning from the window, she began to wander around the room. A small, delicate-looking woman in an oversized flannel shirt and baggy jeans, she always dressed comfortably in private to rest from being the scrupulously groomed, coolly professional public woman. Julia Summers prided herself on the image she presented to publishers, television audiences, the celebrities she interviewed. She was pleased by her skill in interviews, finding out what she needed to know about others while they learned very little about her.

Her press kit informed anyone who wanted to know that she had grown up in Philadelphia, an only child of two successful lawyers. It granted the information that she had attended Brown University, and that she was a single parent. It listed her professional accomplishments, her awards. But it didn't speak of the hell she had lived through in the three years before her parents had divorced, or the fact that she had brought her son into the world alone at age eighteen. There was no mention of the grief she had felt when she had lost her mother, then her father within two years of each other in her mid-twenties.

Though she had never made a secret of it, it was far from common knowledge that she had been adopted when she was six weeks old, and that nearly eighteen years to the day after had given birth to a baby boy whose father was listed on the birth certificate as unknown.

Julia didn't consider the omissions lies—though, of course, she had known the name of Brandon's father. The simple fact was, she was too smooth an interviewer to be trapped into revealing anything she didn't wish to reveal.

And, amused by being able so often to crack façades, she enjoyed being the public Ms. Summers who wore her dark blond hair in a sleek French twist, who chose trim, elegant suits in jewel tones, who could appear on *Donahue* or *Carson* or *Oprah* to tout a new book without showing a trace of the hot, sick nerves that lived inside the public package.

When she came home, she wanted only to be Julia. Brandon's mother. A woman who liked cooking her son's dinner, dusting furniture, planning a garden. Making a home was her most vital work and writing made it possible.

Now, as she waited for her son to come bursting in the door to tell her all about sledding with the neighbors, she thought of the offer her agent had just called her about. It had come out of the blue.

Eve Benedict.

Still pacing restlessly, Julia picked up and replaced knickknacks, plumped pillows on the sofa, rearranged magazines. The living room was a lived-in mess that was more her doing than Brandon's. As she fiddled with the position of a vase of dried flowers or the angle of a china dish, she stepped over kicked-off shoes, ignored a basket of laundry yet to be folded. And considered.

Eve Benedict. The name ran through her head like magic. This was not merely a celebrity, but a woman who had earned the right to be called star. Her talent and her temperament were as well known and as well respected as her face. A face, Julia thought, that had graced movie screens for almost fifty years, in over a hundred films. Two Oscars, a Tony, four husbands—those were only a few of the awards that lined her trophy case. She had known the Hollywood of Bogart and Gable; she had survived, even triumphed, in the days when the studio system gave way to the accountants.

After nearly fifty years in the spotlight, this would be Benedict's first authorized biography. Certainly it was the first time the star had contacted an author and offered her complete cooperation. With strings, Julia reminded herself, and sunk onto the couch. It was those strings that had forced her to tell her agent to stall.

She thrilled with her "V" series. She dazzled with her "Charm Bracelet" trilogy. Now, following nine consecutive national bestsellers, Jane Feather takes on readers' favorite topic with the first novel in an enthralling "bride" trilogy.

The Hostage Bride
BY *JANE FEATHER*

Bride #1 is the outspoken Portia. . . . It's bad enough that seventeen-year-old Portia Worth is taken in by her uncle, the marquis of Granville, after her father dies. As the bastard niece, Portia knows she can expect little beyond a roof over her head and a place at the table. But it truly adds insult to injury when the Granville's archenemy, the outlaw Rufus Decatur, hatches a scheme to abduct the marquis's daughter—only to kidnap Portia by accident. Portia, who possesses more than a streak of independence as well as a talent for resistance, does not take kindly to being abducted—mistakenly or otherwise. Decatur will soon find himself facing the challenge of his life, both on the battle-field and in the bedroom, as he contends with this misfit of a girl who has the audacity to believe herself the equal of any man. . . .

"Now just who do we have here?"

Portia drew the reins tight. The quivering horse raised its head and neighed in protest, pawing the ground. Portia looked up and into a pair of vivid blue eyes glinting with an amusement to match the voice.

"And who are you?" she demanded. "And why have you taken those men prisoner?"

Her hood had fallen back in her struggles with the horse and Rufus found himself the object of a fierce green-eyed scrutiny from beneath an unruly tangle of hair as orange-red as a burning brazier. Her complexion was white as milk, but not from fear, he decided; she looked far too annoyed for alarm.

"Rufus Decatur, Lord Rothbury, at your service," he said solemnly, removing his plumed hat with a flourish as he offered a mock bow from atop his great chestnut stallion. "And who is it who travels under the Granville standard? If you please . . ." He raised a bushy red eyebrow.

Portia didn't answer the question. "Are you abducting us? Or is it murder you have in mind?"

"Tell you what," Rufus said amiably, catching her mount's bridle just below the bit. "We'll trade questions. But let's continue this fascinating but so far uninformative exchange somewhere a little less exposed to this ball-breaking cold."

Portia reacted without thought. Her whip hand rose and she slashed at Decatur's wrist, using all her force so that the blow cut through the leather gauntlet. He gave a shout of surprise, his hand falling from the bridle, and Portia had gathered the reins, kicked at the animal's flanks, and was racing down the track, neither knowing nor caring in which direction, before Rufus fully realized what had happened.

Portia heard him behind her, the chestnut's pounding hooves cracking the thin ice that had formed over the wet mud between the ridges on the track. She urged her horse to greater speed and the animal, still panicked from the earlier melee, threw up his head and plunged forward. If she had given him his head he would have bolted but she hung on, maintaining some semblance of control, crouched low over his neck, half expecting a musket shot from behind.

But she knew this was a race she wasn't going to win. Her horse was a neat, sprightly young gelding, but he hadn't the stride or the deep chest of the pursuing animal. Unless Rufus Decatur decided for some reason to give up the chase, she was going to be overtaken within minutes. And then she realized that her pursuer was not overtaking her, he was keeping an even distance between them, and for some reason this infuriated Portia. It was as if he was playing with her, cat with mouse, allowing her to think she was escaping even as he waited to pounce in his own good time.

She slipped her hand into her boot, her fingers closing over the hilt of the wickedly sharp dagger Jack had insisted she carry from the moment he had judged her mature enough to attract unwelcome attention. By degrees, she drew back on the reins, slowing the horse's mad progress even as she straightened in the saddle. The hooves behind her were closer now. She waited, wanting him to be too close to stop easily. Her mind was cold and clear, her heart steady, her breathing easy. But she was ready to do murder.

With a swift jerk, she pulled up her horse, swinging round in the saddle in the same moment, the dagger in her hand, the weight of the hilt balanced between her index and forefingers, steadied by her thumb.

Rufus Decatur was good and close and as she'd hoped his horse was going fast enough to carry him right past her before he could pull it up. She saw his startled expression as for a minute he was facing her head on. She threw the dagger, straight for his heart.

It lodged in his chest, piercing his thick cloak.

The hilt quivered. Portia, mesmerized, stared at it, for the moment unable to kick her horse into motion again. She had never killed a man before.

"Jesus, Mary, and sainted Joseph!" Rufus Decatur exclaimed in a voice far too vigorous for that of a dead man. He pulled the dagger free and looked down at it in astonishment. "Mother of God!" He regarded the girl on her horse in astonishment. "You were trying to stab me!"

Portia was as astonished as he was, but for rather different reasons. She could see no blood on the blade. And then the mystery was explained. Her intended victim moved aside his cloak to reveal a thickly padded buff coat of the kind soldiers wore. It was fair protection against knives and arrows, if not musket balls.

"You were chasing me," she said, feeling no need to apologize for her murderous intent. Indeed, she sounded as cross as she felt. "You abducted my escort and you were chasing me. Of course I wanted to stop you."

Rufus thought that most young women finding themselves in such a situation, if they hadn't swooned away in fright or thrown a fit of strong hysterics first, would have chosen a less violent course of action. But this tousled and indignant member of the female sex obviously had a rather more down to earth attitude, one with which he couldn't help but find himself in sympathy.

"Well, I suppose you have a point," he agreed, turning the knife over in his hand. His eyes were speculative as he examined the weapon. It was no toy. He looked up, subjecting her to a sharp scrutiny. "I should have guessed that a lass with that hair would have a temper to match."

"As it happens, I don't," Portia said, returning his scrutiny with her own, every bit as sharp and a lot less benign. "I'm a very calm and easy-going person in general. Except when someone's chasing me with obviously malicious intent."

"Well, I have to confess I do have the temper to match," Rufus declared with a sudden laugh as he swept off his hat to reveal his own brightly burnished locks. "But it's utterly dormant at present. All I need from you are the answers to a couple of questions, and then you may be on your way again. I simply want to know who you are and why you're riding under Granville protection."

"And what business is it of yours?" Portia demanded.

"Well . . . you see, anything to do with the Granvilles is my business," Rufus explained almost apologetically. "So, I really do need to have the answers to my questions."

"What are you doing with Sergeant Crampton and his men?"

"Oh, just a little sport," he said with a careless flourish of his hat. "They'll come to no real harm, although they might get a little chilly."

Portia looked over her shoulder down the narrow lane. She could see no sign of either the sergeant and his men or Rufus Decatur's men. "Why didn't you overtake me?" She turned back to him, her eyes narrowed. "You could have done so any time you chose."

"You were going in the right direction so I saw no need," he explained reasonably. "Shall we continue on our way?"

The right direction for what?

In the tradition of *New York Times* bestseller Betina Krahn comes a sparkling new talent with a witty, passionate tale of a spinster wary of desire—and the charming rogue who's determined to change her tune. . . .

The Wedding Chase
BY REBECCA KELLEY

Wolfgang Hardwicke, the Earl of Northcliffe, is up to no good—as usual. So he isn't certain why he rescues the drunken gambler from a fight. And he never expects to be rewarded with a heavenly, all-too-brief glimpse of the gambler's exquisite sister, clad only in her nightgown. Nor does he guess that he'll see her again, lighting up a dull party as she plays piano with an unguardedly rapturous expression—an expression Wolfgang would like to see in decidedly different circumstances. . . . Unlike her admirer, Miss Grizelda Fleetwood is an unabashed do-gooder, one who has as soft a heart for her ne'er-do-well brother as for the unfortunates she helps. Though Zel has no interest in matrimony, she's determined to marry to save her family from financial ruin. That is, if she can find a suitable match before the unprincipled and relentless Earl of Northcliffe ruins her reputation . . . or steals her defenseless heart.

Eventually, Wolfgang found himself in the music room. He hadn't practiced in months but, inspired by Miss Fleetwood's performance, he couldn't resist trying his hand. First the pianoforte, then its player.

A smile brushed his lips. Her sweet blush contrasted so intriguingly with her bold behavior. She followed along with his game of cat and mouse, allowing him to sit far too close, moving away only a bit to encourage rather than discourage him. Yet when faced with competition, she deserted the field, leaving him in Isadora's clutches despite his silent plea for aid.

He sighed, seating himself on the bench. If he wished to be an honorable gentleman, any doubts dictated that he leave her alone. But why should he allow a few scruples to interfere with his amusements? And she did amuse him.

He would proceed with flirtation, moving ever so skillfully into seduction. Smiling, Wolfgang rifled through the sheet music arrayed on the pianoforte. Finding a familiar Mozart sonata, he began to softly finger the hardwood keys.

He was thoroughly destroying the piece when he sensed another presence in the room. A spicy scent. Wolfgang turned to see Grizelda Fleetwood, in another dowdy gown, hesitating at the door. He stopped abruptly, surprised at his embarrassment.

"Discovered! The foul deed uncovered!" He smiled, eased the bench back and stood with a flourish. "I confess my guilt. I've murdered Mozart."

She laughed, a throaty sound of full, easy humor that struck a chord within him. Her laughter bore no resemblance to the rehearsed titter affected by the ladies of the *ton*. "I wouldn't call it murder, my lord, maybe a little unintentional mayhem. You have a fine hand, but it's clear you rarely practice."

"The truth is indeed revealed. I seldom, almost never practice. Lacking discipline, I have become a much better listener than player." Wolfgang took a step closer, drawing her eyes to his. "You are quite beyond my touch."

That faint blush appeared again, as she set a well-worn portfolio on the table. "Do you sight read?"

"About as well as I play."

"That will be fine. I have a few Bach pieces my music master arranged for four hands on the pianoforte." Her low voice softened. "The easier part was for my brother. My part acts as the counterpoint. Would you like to try?"

"I would be honored to take instruction." He bowed, sat back on the bench and patted the seat beside him. "But please be kind to your humble pupil, Madam Music Master."

An answering smile lit her face as she opened her portfolio. She pulled out some tattered papers before sitting a respectable distance from him on the bench. He took the music, scanned it quickly and laid it out where they both could see.

Miss Fleetwood removed her eyeglasses, pushed back a wisp of dark brown hair and ran bare fingers lightly over the keys. "Are you ready? My part joins in after the first few measures."

Wolfgang began to tentatively tap out the notes. The piece was easy and his confidence rapidly increased. Soon she joined in, the notes prancing, circling, interlacing playfully. They both reached to turn the page, his hand met hers, skin to skin. A thrumming—a contralto's lowest note—reverberated through him. Their gazes crossed and locked. Suddenly he wanted to touch much more than her fingers. As if he'd spoken the thought aloud, she looked away, stumbling over the next measure. She seemed to draw herself in, her slender form compact and contained, and continued the piece. He inhaled slowly, breathing in her scent, and found his place in the music, barely missing a note.

As they finished the arrangement, she turned to him with what might have been a smile had her mouth not been so tight. "I believe you could be quite good if you applied yourself."

The corner of his lips twitched as he restrained an answering smile. "I'm always good when I apply myself, Miss Fleetwood." The threatening grin broke through. "But speaking of good, you should see me ride. Do you ride?"

"Ride? What do you . . ." She hesitated slightly. "I ride, but not well."

"Good. I've played your student, now you'll play mine."

On sale in July:

WHEN VENUS FELL
by Deborah Smith

FINDING LAURA
by Kay Hooper

FINDING MR. RIGHT
by Emily Carmichael

Bestselling Historical Women's Fiction

⚹ AMANDA QUICK ⚹

____28354-5 SEDUCTION . . . $6.50/$8.99 Canada

____28932-2 SCANDAL . . . . $6.50/$8.99

____28594-7 SURRENDER . . . . $6.50/$8.99

____29325-7 RENDEZVOUS . . . . $6.50/$8.99

____29315-X RECKLESS . . . . $6.50/$8.99

____29316-8 RAVISHED . . . . $6.50/$8.99

____29317-6 DANGEROUS . . . . $6.50/$8.99

____56506-0 DECEPTION . . . . $6.50/$8.99

____56153-7 DESIRE . . . . $6.50/$8.99

____56940-6 MISTRESS . . . . $6.50/$8.99

____57159-1 MYSTIQUE . . . . $6.50/$7.99

____57190-7 MISCHIEF . . . . $6.50/$8.99

____57407-8 AFFAIR . . . . $6.99/$8.99

⚹ IRIS JOHANSEN ⚹

____29871-2 LAST BRIDGE HOME . . . $5.50/$7.50

____29604-3 THE GOLDEN

BARBARIAN . . . . $6.99/$8.99

____29244-7 REAP THE WIND . . . . . . $5.99/$7.50

____29032-0 STORM WINDS . . . . $6.99/$8.99

Ask for these books at your local bookstore or use this page to order.

Please send me the books I have checked above. I am enclosing $____ (add $2.50 to cover postage and handling). Send check or money order, no cash or C.O.D.'s, please.

Name _____

Address _____

City/State/Zip _____

Send order to: Bantam Books, Dept. FN 16, 2451 S. Wolf Rd., Des Plaines, IL 60018
Allow four to six weeks for delivery.

Prices and availability subject to change without notice.   FN 16 6/98

Bestselling Historical Women's Fiction

❧ IRIS JOHANSEN ❧

____28855-5 THE WIND DANCER . . .$5.99/$6.99
____29968-9 THE TIGER PRINCE . . .$6.99/$8.99
____29944-1 THE MAGNIFICENT
              ROGUE . . . .$6.99/$8.99
____29945-X BELOVED SCOUNDREL .$6.99/$8.99
____29946-8 MIDNIGHT WARRIOR . .$6.99/$8.99
____29947-6 DARK RIDER . . . .$6.99/$8.99
____56990-2 LION'S BRIDE . . . .$6.99/$8.99
____56991-0 THE UGLY DUCKLING. . .$6.99/$8.99
____57181-8 LONG AFTER MIDNIGHT.$6.99/$8.99
____10616-3 AND THEN YOU DIE.... $22.95/$29.95

❧ TERESA MEDEIROS ❧

____29407-5 HEATHER AND VELVET .$5.99/$7.50
____29409-1 ONCE AN ANGEL . . . . . .$5.99/$7.99
____29408-3 A WHISPER OF ROSES .$5.99/$7.99
____56332-7 THIEF OF HEARTS . . . . .$5.50/$6.99
____56333-5 FAIREST OF THEM ALL .$5.99/$7.50
____56334-3 BREATH OF MAGIC . . . .$5.99/$7.99
____57623-2 SHADOWS AND LACE . . .$5.99/$7.99
____57500-7 TOUCH OF ENCHANTMENT. .$5.99/$7.99
____57501-5 NOBODY'S DARLING . . .$5.99/$7.99

- -

Ask for these books at your local bookstore or use this page to order.

Please send me the books I have checked above. I am enclosing $____ (add $2.50 to cover postage and handling). Send check or money order, no cash or C.O.D.'s, please.

Name _____

Address _____

City/State/Zip _____

Send order to: Bantam Books, Dept. FN 16, 2451 S. Wolf Rd., Des Plaines, IL 60018
Allow four to six weeks for delivery.
Prices and availability subject to change without notice.

FN 16 6/98